Tourism English

陳祖昱 著　戴芳美 審閱

全華圖書股份有限公司

Contents

Air Travel

◆Language Functions

Reserving and Confirming a Flight & The Information on an Airplane Ticket and a Boarding Pass & The Regulations of Security Check.

◆Sentence Patterns

Usages of Could & Would, Usages of Would like & Would you like.

◆Vocabulary in Use

Air Travels & Personal items & Information on Passport.

Part 1 Warm Up

Group work! Discuss the following questions in a group.

1 How can you book an air ticket?

I can book an air ticket through
_____, _____, and _____.

Hint
You can book an air ticket through telephoning the travel agency or an airline office, etc.

2 What do you need to ask the airline or travel agency clerk about the flight information?

I need to ask the clerk about the
_____, _____, _____,
_____, and _____ of the flights.

Hint
You need to ask the airline or travel agency clerk about the arrival / departure time, journey, price, etc.

3 What will the clerk ask you about the ticket-booking information?

The clerk might ask me about
my _____, _____, and _____.

Hint
The clerk might ask you about your destination, departure date, one-way / round trip ticket, etc.

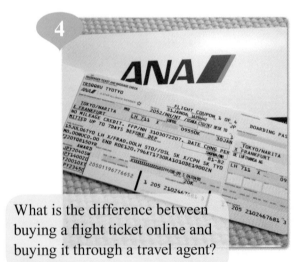

4 What is the difference between buying a flight ticket online and buying it through a travel agent?

Hint
Which one is cheaper? Do you have to pay extra when you buy it from a travel agent?

Part 2 Dialogues

1. Reserving a flight 🎧 003

Reservations clerk: Delta Airlines, good morning. How may I help you?

John Smith: Yes, do you have any flights to San Francisco next Thursday afternoon?

Reservations clerk: One moment, please... Yes. There's a flight at 10:30 and one at 17:00.

John Smith: That's fine. Could you tell me how much a return flight costs? I'll be staying for two weeks.

Reservations clerk: Would that be an economy, business or a first class ticket?

John Smith: Economy, please.

Reservations clerk: That would be a total of US $ 1,450.

John Smith: OK. Could I make a reservation?

Reservations clerk: Certainly. Which flight would you like?

John Smith: The 10:30 one, please.

Reservations clerk: Could I have your name, please?

John Smith: My name is John Smith, that's J-O-H-N S-M-I-T-H.

Reservations clerk: How would you like to pay, Mr. Smith?

John Smith: Can I pay at the check-in desk when I pick up my ticket?

Reservations clerk: Yes, but you will have to confirm this reservation at least two hours before departure time.

John Smith: I see.

Reservations clerk: Now you have been booked, Mr. Smith. The flight leaves at 10:30, and your arrival in San Francisco will be at 18:20, local time. The flight number is Delta7724.

John Smith: Thank you.

Word Bank 🎧 002

flight (n.) 班機
economy (n.) 經濟 (艙)
reservation (n.) 預訂
confirm (v.) 確認
departure (n.) 出發 ; 離開
book (v.) 預訂
arrival (n.) 抵達
local (adj.) 當地的

A Answer the following questions on the basis of the dialogue.

1. What is John Smith doing?
   Check ☑ the correct answer.
   ☐ He is reserving a flight.
   ☐ He is boarding a plane.
   ☐ He is confirming a flight.
2. What is John Smith's destination?
3. What type of ticket would John Smith like?

B Listen to the dialogue again, and then practice with your partner.

2. Confirm a flight  005

Reservations clerk: Delta Airlines. Can I help you?

John Smith: Hello. I'd like to confirm my flight, please.

Reservations clerk: May I have your name and flight number, please?

John Smith: My name is John Smith and my flight number is 7724.

Reservations clerk: When are you leaving?

John Smith: On July 22nd.

Reservations clerk: And your destination?

John Smith: San Francisco.

Reservations clerk: Please hold for a moment. All right. Your seat is confirmed, Mr. Smith. You'll be arriving in San Francisco at 6:20 p.m. local time.

John Smith: Thank you. Can I pick up my ticket when I check in?

Reservations clerk: Yes, but please check in at least one hour before departure time.

Word Bank 004

destination (n.) 目的地
at least (phr.) 至少

A According to the dialogue, how does John Smith confirm his flight. Check ☑ the correct answer.

☐ Call the airline
☐ Visit the airline's website
☐ Visit the airline's ticket counter at the airport

B Discuss the following questions with your partner.

1. Except the way John Smith does, what the other ways that travelers can use to confirm their flight reservations?

2. Except confirming the flight reservation, what other things should we notice after reserving a flight?

Part 3 Sentence Patterns *Usages of Could & Would*

Could/ Would + S.+ V. + O.

Could	I make a reservation?		Certainly. Which flight would you like?
	I have your name, please?		My name is John Smith.
	you tell me how much a return flight costs?		That would be a total of US $ 1,450.
	I have my bill, please?		Just a moment, please.

Would	that be an economy, business or a first class ticket?		Economy, please.

How would	you like to pay, Mr. Smith?		I'll pay at the check-in desk when I pick up my ticket.

A Fill in the blanks with "Would" or "Could".

_____ you wait for a minute?

_____ you do me a favor?

_____ you mind closing the window?

_____ you, please, take me to the manager?

_____ I have a cup of coffee?

_____ someone please answer the phone?

B Use "Could" and "Would" to make polite requests and questions with your partners.

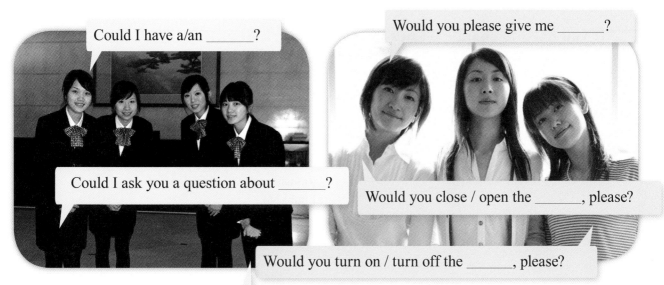

Could I have a/an _____?

Would you please give me _____?

Could I ask you a question about _____?

Would you close / open the _____, please?

Would you turn on / turn off the _____, please?

Could you help me with my _____?

Part 4 Practice

A Booking airline tickets online!

1. Choose one of the airlines provided below, or you may choose an alternative airline if you prefer.
   - Delta Airlines: http://www.delta.com/
   - United Airlines: http://www.united.com/
2. Fill in the following information according to what you find on the Internet in regard to which airline you choose and what flights you take.

Word Bank 007

according to (phr.) 根據
in regard to (phr.) 關於

Your destination: _____ (city, country)

No. of Passengers (Travelers)

_____ Adult (Domestic: ages 18-64, International: ages 12-64)

_____ Child (Domestic: ages 2-17, International: ages 2-11)

_____ Senior (Domestic/ International: age 65 +)

_____ Infant in lap (under 2 yrs.)

_____ Infant in seat (under 2 yrs.)

Route

From (origin): _____
  (city, country)
To (destination): _____
(city, country)
Flight No.: _____
Cabin (service class): _____
Average airfare per person: _____
Date of departure: _____
Time of departure: _____
Date of arrival: _____
Time of arrival: _____

*If you need to change planes

The place you change planes
(transfer city, country): _____

Flight No.: _____
Date of departure: _____
Time of departure: _____
Date of arrival: _____
Time of arrival: _____

Return Flight

Flight No.: _____
Date of departure: _____
Time of departure: _____
Date of arrival: _____
Time of arrival: _____

***If you need to change planes**

The place you change planes
(transfer city, country): _____
Flight No.: _____

B Recognize your passport!

Following is a specimen of R.O.C passport. Work with your partner to give your personal information on Name, Also known as, Nationality, Sex, Date of birth, Place of birth, and Identity No. shown on the passport. To translate your Chinese name into English, you may refer to the website: http://staffweb.ncnu.edu.tw/robert/chinese/transweb/py-ty.htm

Word Bank 🎧008

specimen (n.) 樣本
personal (adj.) 個人的

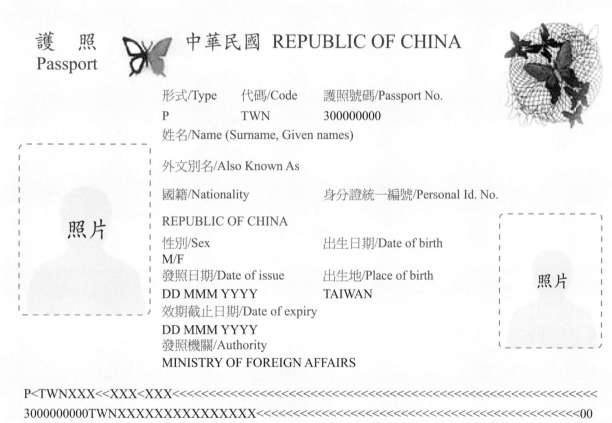

護 照
Passport

中華民國 REPUBLIC OF CHINA

形式/Type   代碼/Code   護照號碼/Passport No.
P   TWN   300000000
姓名/Name (Surname, Given names)

照片

外文別名/Also Known As

國籍/Nationality   身分證統一編號/Personal Id. No.
REPUBLIC OF CHINA

性別/Sex   出生日期/Date of birth
M/F
發照日期/Date of issue   出生地/Place of birth
DD MMM YYYY   TAIWAN
效期截止日期/Date of expiry
DD MMM YYYY
發照機關/Authority
MINISTRY OF FOREIGN AFFAIRS

照片

P<TWNXXX<<XXX<XXX<<<<<<<<<<<<<<<<<<<<<<<<<<<<<<<<<<<<
3000000000TWNXXXXXXXXXXXXXX<<<<<<<<<<<<<<<<<<<<<<<<<<<<<<<<<00

Part 5 Role Play

Pair work! Fill in the blanks and practice the completed dialogue with your partner.

I would like to...

Passenger

Clerk

👤 _____ Airlines. May I help you, _____?

👤 Yes, I'd like to go to _____ next _____.

👤 What time would you like to leave?

👤 I'd like to fly at around _____ next _____.

👤 First class or _____, _____?

👤 _____, please.

👤 Would you like a _____ ticket or a _____ ticket?

👤 _____ ticket, please.

👤 May I have your name and telephone number, _____?

👤 My name is _____, that's _____. Telephone number is _____.

👤 Thank you, _____.

Lesson B *Check in and Security Check*

Part 1 Warm Up

A What documents do you need while checking in at the Airline counter? Please check the correct ones.

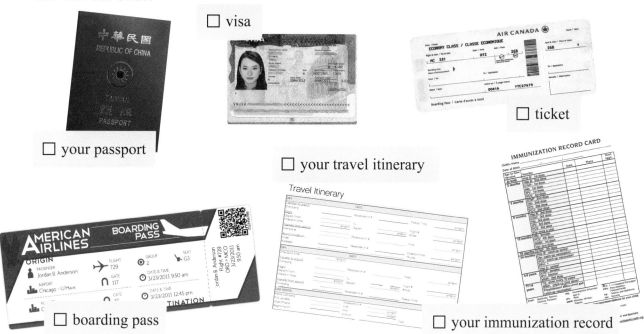

☐ visa

☐ ticket

☐ your passport

☐ your travel itinerary

☐ boarding pass

☐ your immunization record

B What items will be checked while passing through airport security check points? Please check the correct ones.

☐ boarding pass and/or ticket

☐ any items in your pockets (keys, cell phones)

☐ identification

☐ laptops

☐ PDAs

☐ all liquids and gels

☐ shoes

Part 2 Dialogues

1.At the airline counter 🎧 010

Agent: Hello, may I ask where are you flying today, please?

David: Of course, I'm flying to Prague.

Agent: Can I see your passport and ticket, please?

David: Certainly. There you go.

Agent: Great! Would you like a window or aisle seat?

David: I'd like a window seat, please.

Agent: All right and how many pieces of baggage do you have with you today?

David: I have one baggage and one carry-on suitcase.

Agent: Okay, please put your baggage on the scale. (Weighs baggage) There you go.

A Answer the following questions on the basis of the dialogue.

1. Which country is David flying to?

☐ Germany   ☐ Czech Republic

☐ France   ☐ U. S. A

> **Word Bank** 🎧 009
>
> piece (n.) 件
> baggage (n.) 行李
> carry-on suitcase (n.)
> 隨身手提箱
> weigh (v.) 秤重量
> scale (n.) 秤

2. How many pieces of baggage does David bring with him?

B Listen to the dialogue again and then practice with your partner.

2.At the security checkpoint 🎧 012

Security Guard: May I see your passport and boarding pass, please?
David: Sure, here you go.
Security Guard: Thank you. Do you have anything with metal on you? Any change in your wallet, watches, jewelry, or a belt? If so, please take them off and put them into the bin.
David: Okay. Here you go and here's my belt.
Security Guard: Do you have any liquids, gels, pastes, creams or aerosols?
David: I only have this bottle of cranberry juice that I just bought.
Security Guard: Sorry, but you're only allowed a 3.4 ounce (100ml) bottle or less, so please drink it up now or throw it away.
David: But I can't guzzle all this.
Security Guard: I'm sorry then, you'll have to throw it away.
David: Okay, fine.

A **What items cannot be carried on an airplane? Check ☑ the correct answer**

□ watch
□ jewelry
□ large baggage
□ carry-on suitcase
□ toothpaste
□ suntan lotion
□ lighters and matches

Word Bank 🎧 011

metal (n.) 金屬
wallet (n.) 錢包
jewelry (n.) 珠寶
bin (n.) 箱子
liquids (n.) 液體
gels (n.) 凝膠
pastes (n.) 膏
aerosols (n.) 氣霧劑
cranberry (n.) 蔓越橘；小紅莓
guzzle (v.) (n.) 牛飲；暴食

B Listen to the dialogue again and then practice with your partner.

Part 3 Sentence Patterns *Usage of Would like* 013

S. + would like + O. / to V.

| I would (=I'd) like | something to drink.
two kilos of tomatoes, please.
to watch a movie.
to visit that museum. |

Would + S. + like + O. / to V.

| Would you like | a window or aisle seat?
something to drink?
to go for a walk?
to join us? | I'd like a window seat, please.
Yes, orange juice, please.
Sure, let's go now.
Yes, that's great. |

A Unscramble the following sentences.

1. would/ she/ to/ like/ go/ vacation/ on / this/ year. _____.
2. He/ meet/ wouldn't/ to/ you/ like. _____.
3. wouldn't/ to/ swim/ there/ I/ like. _____.
4. Ann / get / would / a ticket / like / for a concert/ to? _____?
5. some/ would/ like/ Tom/ eat/ to/ sandwiches _____?

B Use "I would like…" and "Would you like…" to make sentences with your partners.

Part 4 Practice

A Recognize an airline ticket

Regardless of the type, all airline tickets contain details of the following information: the passenger's name, the issuing airline, a ticket number including the airline's 3 digit code at the start of the number, the cities the ticket is valid for travel between, flights that the ticket is valid for, baggage allowance, taxes, the fare basis, an alpha-numeric code that identifies the fare, restrictions on changes and refunds, dates that the ticket is valid for, and form of payment, details of how the ticket was paid for.

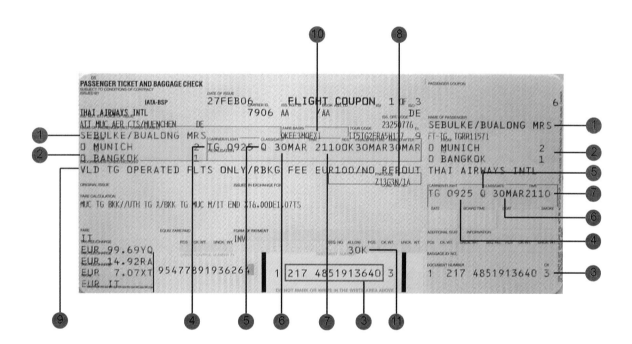

1 Passenger's Name
2 Route
3 Ticket Number
4 Flight Number
5 Ticket Booking Class
6 Date of Journey
7 Local Departure Time
8 Ticket Reservation Number
9 Ticket Restrictions/ Endorsements
10 Fare Basis
11 Baggage Allowance

1. What is the airline code for THAI AIR WAYS INTL _____
2. What is the traveler's destination? _____
3. What time does the passenger leave Munich? _____
4. What is the free baggage allowance? _____

B Recognize a boarding pass

A boarding pass is a document provided by an airline during check-in, giving a passenger permission to board the airplane for a particular flight. As a minimum, it identifies the passenger, the flight number, and the date and scheduled time for departure. Generally, the gate that is scheduled for boarding is also included.

1. Where is the passenger going? _____
2. What is the passenger's gate number? _____
3. What is the boarding time? _____

Part 5 Role Play

Work in pairs. Take turns with your partner to play the roles of a security officer and a passenger. Practice the following commands and questions at the Security Checkpoint.

Command 1

Boarding pass, please.

Command 2

ID please. (show your photo ID)

Command 3

Spread your arms out, please. (Put your arms up and out to the sides of your body)

Command 4

Take your shoes off.

Command 5

Open your bag.

Command 6

Take off/remove your belt.

Question1 Do you have any change in your pockets?
Question2 Do you have any metals?
Question3 Do you have any food/produce?
Question4 Do you have any liquids or medicine?

Command 7

You must dump all food or beverages. (You can't bring it through the gates.)

Command 8

Walk through.

Tips for Reserving Airline Tickets Online 014

1. To get the cheapest flight tickets online, make sure that you book the tickets at least 3 weeks in advance.
2. Research airlines for the best flights and best fares.
3. Log on to your airline's website.
4. Check the box indicating which type of travel you prefer, round trip or one way.
5. Enter your departure city, destination, departure date, return date, and number of passengers. Click "Continue".
6. Choose your flights from the search options provided and click "Continue".
7. Enter your passenger information in the boxes provided and click "Continue".
8. Enter your credit card information and click "Continue".
9. Confirm your information and click "Submit".

Sentence Completion

( ) 1. Please remember to call the airline directly to _____ your flight.
(A) affirm   (B) assure   (C) confirm   (D) guarantee

( ) 2. If you want to find the cheapest airplane ticket, _____ can usually be found through the Internet.
(A) bargains   (B) destinations   (C) reservations   (D) itinerary

( ) 3. When you arrive at the airport, the first thing you do is go to _____.
(A) the departure lounge   (B) the check-in desk   (C) the arrival desk   (D) the customs

( ) 4. When I take a flight, I always ask for _____ seat, so it is easier for me to get up and walk around.
(A) a window   (B) a cabinet   (C) a middle   (D) an aisle

( ) 5. The flight is scheduled to _____ at eleven o'clock tomorrow. You will have to get to the airport two hours before the takeoff.
(A) land   (B) depart   (C) cancel   (D) examine

Tips for Waiting for your Flight 🎧 015

1. If you lose your way, don't get desperate. Many people can help you at the airport.
2. If you have some extra time, wait in front of your gate until it opens.
3. All major airports offer many shops and displays, so don't be afraid to look around and explore. Just keep an eye on your watch.
4. Never leave your stuff alone, always have it with you.

Sentence Completion

(　) 1. You will get a boarding _____ after completing the check-in.
   (A) pass　　　　　(B) post　　　(C) plan　　　(D) past

(　) 2. Beware of strangers at the airport and do not leave your luggage _____.
   (A) unanswered　(B) uninterested　(C) unimportant　(D) unattended

(　) 3. The flight to Chicago has been _____ due to heavy snow.
   (A) concealed　(B) cancelled　(C) compared　(D) consoled

(　) 4. You will need to take a _____ flight from Taoyuan to Kaohsiung.
   (A) contacting　(B) connecting　(C) competing　(D) computing

(　) 5. Passengers _____ to other airlines should report to the information desk on the second floor.
   (A) have transferred　(B) transfer　(C) are transferred　(D) transferring

In-Flight and Immigration

◆Language Functions

In-flight Announcements & Transferring & Immigration

◆Sentence Patterns

Simple Present Passive Voice & How long

◆Vocabulary in Use

U.S. Form I-94 & Customs Declaration Form & Baggage claim

Part 1 Warm Up

A Discuss the following questions in a group.

1. Can you use your cell phone during the flight? Why?

2. Can you smoke in the aircraft bathroom? Why?

3. What should you do if the cabin is experiencing the pressure loss?

B Circle what you cannot take onboard a flight.

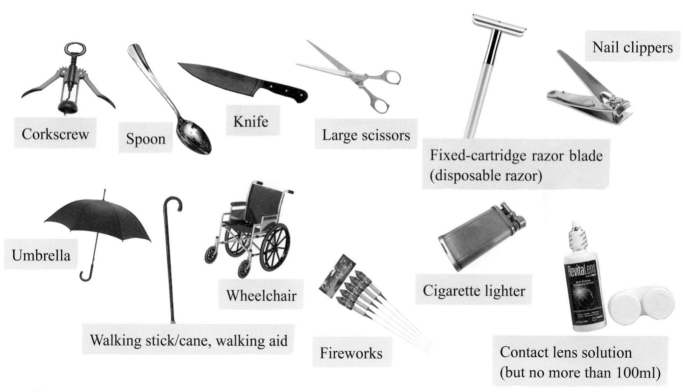

Corkscrew

Spoon

Knife

Large scissors

Nail clippers

Fixed-cartridge razor blade (disposable razor)

Umbrella

Wheelchair

Walking stick/cane, walking aid

Fireworks

Cigarette lighter

Contact lens solution (but no more than 100ml)

Part 2 Dialogues

1. In-flight Announcement (Before Takeoff) 017

Word Bank 016

be bound for (phr.) 前往
reminder (n.) 提醒者；提醒物
securely (adv.) 安全地
overhead (adj.) 在上頭的
compartments (n.) 置物櫃
in front of (phr.) 在...之前
captain (n.) 船長；艦長；(飛機的) 機長
approximately (adv.) 大概；近乎
fasten (v.) 繫緊
straighten (v.) 使挺直
refrain from (phr.) 避免
electronic (adj.) 電子的
devices (n.) 設備
allow (v.) 允許
cooperation (n.) 合作
appreciate (v.) 感謝
pleasant (adj.) 愉快的

Ladies and gentlemen, this is United Airlines Flight 203 bound for Los Angeles. While you are getting comfortable in the cabin, this is a reminder that all carry-on luggage must fit securely either in the overhead compartments or under the seat directly in front of you. The captain of this flight is Mr. Frank Davies. Today's flight time will be approximately 13 hours. Let us remind you to fasten your seat belts and straighten your seats. Also, please refrain from smoking at all times during the flight. The use of cell phones and other personal electronic devices is not allowed at any time. Your cooperation will be much appreciated. If there is anything we can do for you, please let us know. We wish you a pleasant flight. Thank you.

A Answer the following questions on the basis of the announcement.

1. Where is the flight flying to?
2. Where can you put your carry-on luggage?
3. How long will be the flying time?

B Listen to this announcement again and then read it!

2. In-flight Announcement (Safety Briefing) 019

Ladies and gentlemen, on behalf of the crew I ask that you please direct your attention to the monitors in front of you as we review the emergency procedures. There are eight emergency exits on this aircraft. Please take a minute to locate the emergency exit closest to you. Note that the nearest exit may be behind you. Should the cabin experience sudden pressure loss, stay calm and listen for instructions from the cabin crew. Oxygen masks will drop down from above your seat. Place the mask over your mouth and nose, like this. Pull the strap to tighten it. If you are traveling with small children, make sure that you secure your own mask first before helping your children with theirs. In the unlikely event of an emergency landing and evacuation, life rafts are located below your seats and emergency lighting will lead you to your closest emergency exit. We ask that you make sure that all carry-on bags are stowed away safely during the flight. While we wait for take-off, please take a moment to review the airline safety sheet in the seat pocket in front of you.

Word Bank 018

on behalf of (phr.) 代表
crew (n.) 全體機員
monitors (n.) 顯示器
emergency (n.) 緊急情況
locate (v.) 找出
experience (v.) 經歷
pressure (n.) 壓力
loss (n.) 喪失；減低
calm (adj.) 鎮靜的
oxygen masks (n.) 氧氣罩
tighten (v.) 繫緊
evacuation (n.) 撤離
life rafts (n.) 救生筏

A Circle the items you hear from the announcement.

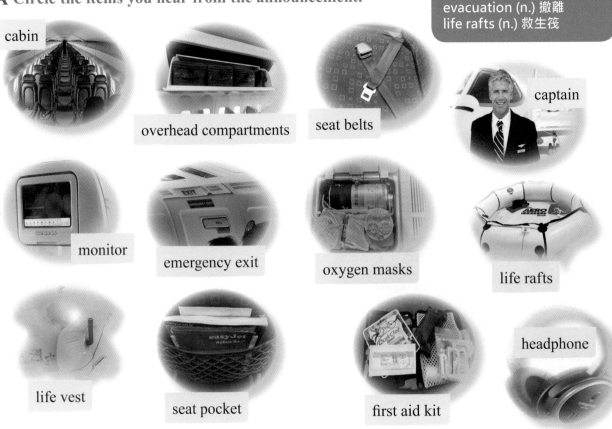

cabin

overhead compartments

seat belts

captain

monitor

emergency exit

oxygen masks

life rafts

life vest

seat pocket

first aid kit

headphone

B Listen to the announcement again. Then read it!

Part 3 Sentence Patterns   *Simple Present Passive Voice* 020

S. + to be (not) + V. (past participle)

Life rafts are located below your seats.
The use of cell phones and other personal electronic devices is not allowed at any time.
All carry-on bags are stowed away safely during the flight.
Water is drunk by everyone.

A Rewrite the sentences in passive voice.

1. Michelle opens the window.
  → The window is opened by her.

2. We set the table.
  → _____

3. Amy pays a lot of money.
  → _____

4. The policemen help the children.
  → _____

5. Mary does the housework.
  → _____

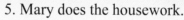

B Work with your partners to make four sentences with simple present passive voice.

_____

_____

_____

_____

Part 4 Practice

Fill it in! Imagine you are going through the U. S. customs checkpoint. Complete the following U.S. Form I-94.

I-94 Arrival/Departure Record – Instructions

This form must be completed by all persons except U. S. Citizens, returning resident aliens, aliens with immigrant visas, and Canadian Citizens visiting or in transit.

Type or print legibly with pen in ALL CAPITAL LETTERS. Use English. Do not write on the back of this form.

This form is in two parts. Please complete both the Arrival Record (Items 1 through 13) and the Departure Record (Items 14 through 17).

When all items are completed, present this form to the CBP Officer.

Item 7 – If you are entering the United States by land, enter **LAND** in this space.

If you are entering the United States by ship, enter **SEA** in this space.

Admission Number

287377018 18

Arrival Record

1. Family Name

2. First (Given) Name

3. Birth Date(Day/Mo/Yr)

4. Country of Citizenship

5. Sex (Male or Female)

6. Passport Number

7. Airline and Flight Number

8. Country Where You Live

9. City Where You Boarded

10. City where Visa was Issued

11. Date Issued(Day/Mo/Yr)

12. Address While in the United States (Number and Street)

13. City and State

287377018 18

I-94
Departure Record

14. Family Name

15. First (Given) Name

16. Birth Date (Day/Mo/Yr)

17. Country of Citizenship

CBP Form I-94 (10/04)

STAPLE HERE

See Other Side

Part 5 Role Play

Pair work! Fill in the blanks and then practice the completed dialogue with your partner.

Destination	Connecting Flight
New York	US Airways Flight 6100
Paris	EVA Airways 87
Edinburgh	British Airways 1472
Washington D.C	All Nippon Flight 1083
Prague	Czech Airlines 4629

May I see your ticket and passport?

Yes, there you are.

I just came in on EVA flight _____. My destination is _____. Do I need to change planes to _____?

The ticket says that you're connecting with _____ to _____ on the same day. It means you have to change to another flight at _____. Let me take care of it for you. Here, this is your new boarding pass with the seat number on it. Please board at Gate _____ for _____.

What about my luggage?

All of your checked luggage will be automatically transferred to the connecting flight _____.

That's perfect, thank you.

Part 1 Warm Up

A Listen to these three people, and fill in the following blanks with what you hear. 021

I am a _____ and I am here for _____.
I plan to stay here for _____.

I am a _____ and I am going to _____ in
Los Angeles. I plan to stay here for _____.

I am a _____ and I am here for _____. I
plan to stay here for _____.

B Read the following passage, then complete the questions.

Immigration or immigration control is the place at a port, airport, or international border where officials check the passports of people who wish to come into the country. The immigration officers may ask some questions, try to answer the following questions and practice with your partner.

1. What's the nature of your visit? (= What's the purpose of your visit?)
   I am here for _____.

> **Hint**
> business, employment, immigration, studying, sightseeing, attending a conference, visiting a friend, etc.

2. What's your occupation? (= What do you do?)
   I'm a / an _____

3. How long do you plan to stay in the United States?
   For _____

> **Hint**
> days, weeks, months

Part 2 Dialogues 023

1. Immigration Control

Immigration officer: Good evening. Where have you come from?

John Smith: Taipei, Taiwan.

Immigration officer: May I have your passport and form I-94, please?

John Smith: Here you are.

Immigration officer: What's the nature of your visit? Business or pleasure?

John Smith: Pleasure. I'm visiting my friends.

Immigration officer: How long are you going to stay in the United States?

John Smith: Two weeks.

Immigration officer: What is your occupation?

John Smith: I work as an engineer for a computer company.

Immigration officer: Do you have a return ticket?

John Smith: Yes, here it is.

Immigration officer: That's fine. Thanks. Enjoy your trip.

John Smith: Thank you.

Word Bank 022

occupation (n.) 職業

A Answer the following questions on the basis of the dialogue.

1. Where is John flying from?
2. What is John going to do in the United States?
3. What does John do?

B Listen to the dialogue again, and then practice with your partner.

2. Baggage Claim 025

Passenger: Excuse me but do you know what baggage carousel the bags from Delta Flight 7724 are on?

Airport Worker: Yes, I believe they are on carousel 9. But you should check the monitors to make sure.

Passenger: Thanks so much for your time.

Airport Worker: Not a problem, sir.

Word Bank 024

baggage carousel (n.) 行李運輸帶

A **Answer the following questions on the basis of the dialogue.**

1. What is the passenger's problem?
2. What is the airport worker's suggestion?

B **Listen to the dialogue again, and then practice with your partner.**

Part 3 Sentence Patterns *How long...* 🎧026

How long + Auxiliary V. + S. + V.

Q :

How long	are	you	going to stay	in the United States?
	have	you	been waiting?	
	will	the concert	last?	
	have	they	been married?	

A :

- Two weeks.
- Only for a minute or two.
- It should be over by nine o'clock.
- More than 18 years.

A Look at the following short dialogues. Fill in the gaps in the questions using the verb in brackets.

1. A: My father is a doctor.
   B: How long (be) _____
   _____ a doctor?
   A: Twenty-two years.

2. A: We spent our holiday in San Diego last year.
   B: How long (spend) _____ there?
   A: Only two weeks. It wasn't really long enough to see everything.

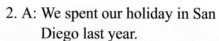

3. A: I work for a computer company in Los Angeles.
   B: How long _____ (work) for them?
   A: eight years.

4. A: I drove to San Francisco yesterday.
   B: How long (take) _____ you to get there?
   A: About four hours - there was a lot of traffic on the roads.

5. A: I can't send any emails, my computer's broken.
   B: How long (be) _____ broken?
   A: About a week. I'm going to take it back to the shop when I get time.

B Now ask your partner three questions by using "How long…?"

Part 4 Practice

Fill it in! Complete the Customs Declaration Form.

Customs Declaration

Each arriving traveler or responsible family member must provide the following information (only ONE written declaration per family is required):

1. Family Name

   First (Given)   Middle

2. Birth date   Day   Month   Year

3. Number of Family members traveling with you

4. (a) U.S. Street Address (hotel name / destination)

   (b) City   (c) State

5. Passport issued by (country)

6. Passport number

7. Country of Residence

8. Countries visited on this

   trip prior to U.S. arrival

9. Airline / Flight No. or Vessel Name

10. The primary purpose of this trip is business: Yes ☐   No ☐

11. I am (We are) bringing:
    (a) fruit, plants, food, insect   Yes ☐   No ☐
    (b) meats, animals, animal / wildlife products   Yes ☐   No ☐
    (c) disease agents, cell cultures, snails   Yes ☐   No ☐
    (d) soil or have been on a farm / ranch / pasture.   Yes ☐   No ☐

12. I have (We have) been in close proximity of (such as touching or handling) livestock: Yes ☐   No ☐

13. I am (We have) carrying currency or monetary instruments over $10,000 U.S. or foreign equivalent   Yes ☐   No ☐

14. I have (We have) commercial merchandise: Yes ☐   No ☐
    (articles for sale, samples used for soliciting orders, or goods that are not considered personal effects)

15. Residents: the total value of all goods, including commercial merchandise I / we have purchased or acquired abroad, (including gifts for someone else, but not items mailed to the U.S.) and am / are bringing to the U.S. is : $
    Visitors: the total value of all articles that will remain in the U.S., including commercial merchandise is:
    $

I HAVE READ THE IMPORTANT INFORMATION ON THIS FORM AND HAVE MADE A TRUTHFUL DECLARATION:

X _____

              (Signature)   Date (day/month/year)

Part 5 Role Play

A Take turns to play the roles of a customs and immigration officer at an airport and tourists from different countries.

1. Welcome to _____.
2. May I see your passport?
3. Where are you coming from?
4. What is the purpose of your visit?
5. How long are you planning to stay?
6. Where will you be staying?
7. Is this your first time to _____?
8. Do you have anything to declare?
9. Enjoy your stay.

B Record the description what you hear from your classmates.

Name	Nationality	Last Country Visited	Purpose of Visit

Intended Length of Stay	Location of Stay	Anything to Declare	First Time (Y/N)

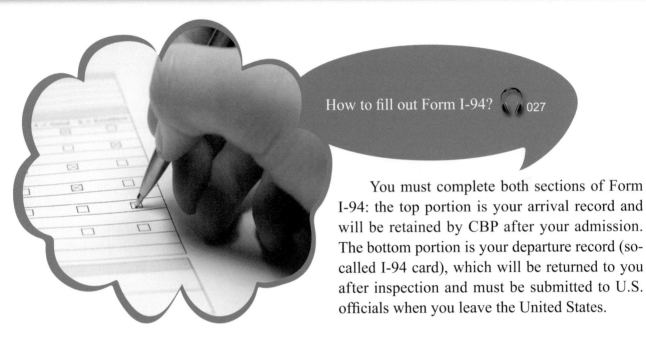

How to fill out Form I-94? 🎧 027

You must complete both sections of Form I-94: the top portion is your arrival record and will be retained by CBP after your admission. The bottom portion is your departure record (so-called I-94 card), which will be returned to you after inspection and must be submitted to U.S. officials when you leave the United States.

To fill out the form you will need the following information:
- Your Name, DOB, Nationality, Sex (Male or Female), Country of Residence and Passport Number;
- Airline and Flight Number, if you flew to the US;
- The city where you boarded the flight;
- The city where your visa was issued;
- The date when your visa was issued; and
- The address where you will stay in the U.S.

CBP officials will stamp the I-94 card, and write down your immigration status and authorized period of stay, before returning it to you.

Fill it in! Complete the following dialogue with the correct word or phrase in the box.

| white | coke | beef | enjoy | perfect |

Attendant: Would you like chicken or _____?
Passenger: I'd like chicken, please. Is it dark meat or _____ meat?
Attendant: It's white meat. Is that okay ?
Passenger: Yeah, that's _____.
Attendant: Here you are.
Passenger: Thank you. And could I please have a _____?
Attendant: Most definitely you can. _____ your meal ma'am.

Go through U.S. customs 028

Tips
● Be nice to the officers. Most likely they will return the favor.
● Make sure you have all of the required forms completed before you present them to the Passport Control or Customs officer.
● Often times there will be another officer at the very front of the Passport Control line directing you to the next open booth. The booths are also numbered to help you.
● Do not worry about getting lost. Just follow the signs as there is only one way through these facilities.

Warnings
● Photography, smoking, and cell phone usage is never allowed in U.S Customs and Immigration facilities. No calling, no texting - Remember that you are inside a highly secure federal government facility.
● Once you leave the baggage claim/customs area you may not re-enter, so be sure you have all of your personal belongings with you before you leave for the connecting flights or international arrivals area.
● As always, never make jokes about bombing, terrorism, smuggling, etc., as they are required to take all threats seriously.

Fill it in! **Complete the sentences with the correct word or phrase in the box.**

| lost and found | currency exchange | restroom | elevators | baggage claim |

1. Passengers can take _____ or escalators up to the food court at the terminal 1.
2. Can you keep an eye on my bags while I go to the _____?
3. We found your spectacles but they have been taken to the _____ department.
4. You can get your checked baggage back at the _____ area.
5. Adeline is going to the bank or _____ office over there to change her British pounds into U.S. dollars.

Asking and Giving Directions

◆ **Language Functions**

Asking Directions & Giving Directions

◆ **Sentence Patterns**

Asking Directions and Giving Directions

◆ **Vocabulary in Use**

Traffic terms

Part 1 Warm Up

A Listen to the following talks, and complete the sentences. 029

_____ I get to the British Museum?
Go straight down the street and you will come to a fork in the road, and turn right. It's on your right side.

_____, but _____ tell me the way to the Metropolitan Museum?
Yes, turn right at the third intersection. It's just right on the corner.

_____ does it take to walk from here to the Lincoln Aquarium?
Just walk down this street. It takes about 15 minutes. It's on your left-hand side.

_____ tell me the way to the nearest bank?
Go three blocks to the corner of Lincoln Avenue and 40th Street, and it's on the right side.

B When you ask someone for directions, what might you say? Check ☑ the correct answers.

☐ How do I get to Main Street?
☐ I'm looking for Jane Street.
☐ Can you tell me where the community center is?

☐ Where is the closest gas station?
☐ Do you want me to draw you a map?

Part 2 Dialogues 031

James: Excuse me, I'm afraid I can't find a bank. Do you know where one is?

Passerby: Well, there are a few banks near here. Do you have a particular bank in mind?

James: I'm afraid I don't. I just need to withdraw some money from either a teller or an ATM.

Passerby: OK, that's easy.

James: I'm going by car.

Passerby: Well, in that case, go straight ahead on this street until the third traffic light. Take a left there, and continue on until you come to a stop sign.

James: Do you know what the name of the street is?

Passerby: Yes, I think it's Maple Street. Now, when you come to the stop sign, take the street on the left. You'll be on 5th Avenue.

James: OK, I go straight ahead on this street to the third traffic light. That's Maple Street.

Passerby: Yes, that's right.

James: Then I continue on to the stop sign and take a right on 5th Avenue.

Passerby: No, take a left at the stop sign onto 5th Avenue.

James: Oh, thanks. What's next?

Passerby: Well, continue on 5th Avenue for about 150 yards, past a supermarket until you come to another traffic light. Take a left and continue on for another 150 yards. You'll see the bank on the right.

James: Well, thank you very much for taking the time to explain this to me!

Passerby: Not at all. Enjoy your visit!

James: Thank you.

> **Word Bank** 🎧 030
>
> particular (adj.) 特定的
> withdraw (v.) 提取
> straight (adv.) 直接地，一直地
> ATM = Automated Teller Machine,
> Automatic Teller Machine (n.) 自動
> 存提款機
> traffic light (n.) 紅綠燈；交通指揮燈

A For each sentence, check ☑ T (true) or F (false)

James is looking for City Bank.	T ☐	F ☐
James is going to deposit his money in a bank.	T ☐	F ☐
James is asking for directions on a bus.	T ☐	F ☐
The bank is on Maple Street.	T ☐	F ☐

B Listen to the dialogue again, and then practice with your partner.

Part 3 Sentence Patterns *Asking Directions* 032

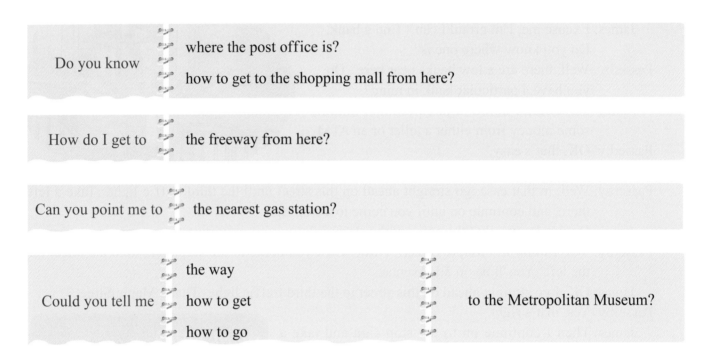

| Do you know | where the post office is? |
| | how to get to the shopping mall from here? |

| How do I get to | the freeway from here? |

| Can you point me to | the nearest gas station? |

Could you tell me	the way
	how to get	to the Metropolitan Museum?
	how to go

A Complete the following sentences.

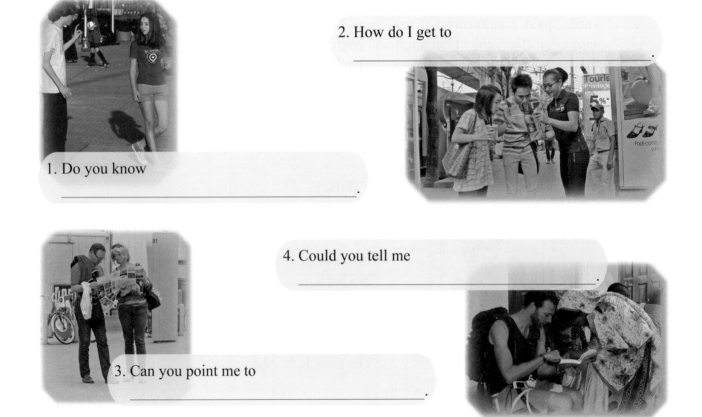

2. How do I get to
_____.

1. Do you know
_____.

4. Could you tell me
_____.

3. Can you point me to
_____.

B Now work with your partners to use the completed sentences to ask directions.

Part 4 Practice

Identify the location! Look at the map and use the prepositions in the box to fill the following sentences.

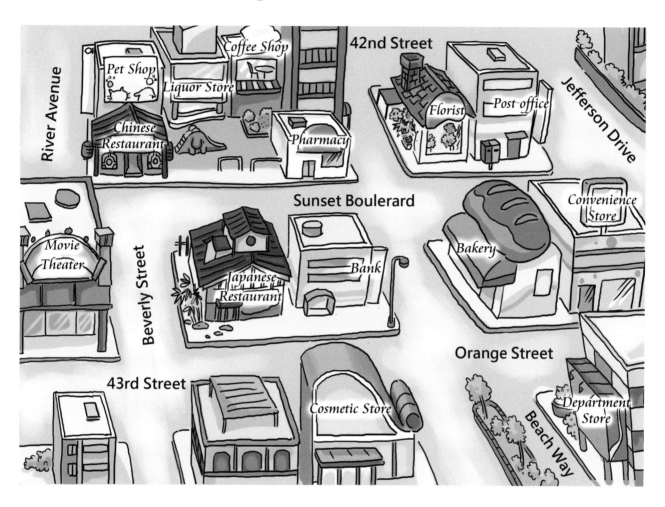

opposite	between	on	in front	behind
next	beside	across	on the right	on the corner

1. The pet shop is _____ the Chinese restaurant.
2. The Bank is _____ Sunset Boulevard.
3. The Post Office is _____ of the Florist.
4. The Movie Theater is _____ from the Japanese Restaurant.
5. The Department Store is _____ the Convenience Store.
6. The Bank is _____ to the Japanese Restaurant.
7. The Liquor Store is _____ the Pet Shop.
8. The Liquor Store is _____ the Pet Shop and the Coffee Shop.
9. The Movie Theater is _____ of Sunset Boulevard and Beverly Street.
10. The Chinese Restaurant is _____ the Pet Shop.

Part 5 Role Play

A fill in the following dialogue with the questions in the box.

> Yes, I can see them.
> Thank you. That's very kind of you.
> Maybe I should call a taxi.
> Excuse me, can you help me? I'm lost!
> I'd like to go to the museum, but I can't find it. Is it far?

Tourist: _____.
Person: Certainly, where would you like to go?
Tourist: _____.
Person: No, not really. It's about a 5 minute walk.
Tourist: _____.
Person: No, no. It's very easy. Really. I can give you directions.
Tourist: _____.
Person: Not at all.... Now, go along this street to the traffic lights. Do you see them?
Tourist: _____.
Person: Right, at the traffic lights, turn left into Queen Mary Avenue.
Tourist: Queen Mary Avenue.
Person: Right. Go straight on. Take the second left and enter Museum Drive.
Tourist: OK. Queen Mary Avenue, straight on and then the third left, Museum Drive.
Person: No, it's the second left.

B Practice the completed dialogue with your partner.

Giving Directions

Part 1 Warm Up

A Listen to the following talks, and complete the sentences. 🎧 033

Will you tell me where the nearest office of China Airlines is?

Yes. _____ this street. It's _____ Adams Street and Fifth Avenue.

Is the MetroWalk Mall far from here?

No, it's not far. Just go _____ down the street. It's about 10 minutes _____.

How far is the Holiday Inn from here?

It's about a twenty-minute _____. You can take No. 5 bus right here.

Is there a short cut to the Metropolitan Museum?

Yes. Just go straight down the street and _____ at the traffic light, and then go straight on for 5 minutes. You will see it on your _____ side.

B When you give someone directions, what might you say? Check the correct answers.

- ☐ It's just around the corner.
- ☐ Turn right at the next street.
- ☐ It's about a twenty minute bus ride.

- ☐ It's about a five minute walk.
- ☐ It's across from the blue church.
- ☐ I'm afraid I can't help you.

Part 2 Dialogues 035

Word Bank 🎧 034

aquarium (n.) 水族館
interrupt (v.) 打斷 (講話)
block (n.) 街區

Jerry: Excuse me. Can you tell me the way to the aquarium?
Pedestrian A: No, I'm sorry. I don't know. I'm from out of town.
　　　　　(A minute later···)
Jerry: Excuse me. Do you know where the aquarium is?
Pedestrian B: Sure. It's not far from here. Walk straight ahead until you get to Main Street. Then...
Jerry: Sorry to interrupt. How many blocks is that?
Pedestrian B: It's about two or three blocks. It's the first traffic light you come to. When you get to Main Street, turn right and walk one block to Broadway. Then turn left and go half a block.
Jerry: Which side of the street is it on?
Pedestrian B: Coming from this direction, it will be on your right side. It's in the middle of the block, next to Central Park. You can't miss it. Do you want me to repeat any of that?
Jerry: No, that's okay. I've got it. Thanks a lot.
Pedestrian B: You're welcome.

A Answer the following questions based on the dialogue above.

1. What is Jerry looking for?
2. Did the pedestrian A know where the aquarium was?
3. How many blocks is the aquarium away from Jerry?
4. Which side of the street is it on coming from their direction?

B Listen to the dialogue again, and then practice with your partner.

Part 3 **Sentence Patterns** *Giving Directions* 036

The easiest / quickest / best way is to⋯
The easiest way is to turn right on Main Street.
Turn right / left
Turn right at the next street / traffic light / third intersection.
Stay on + road name for + distance or time
Stay on Route 1 for about ten minutes.
Go straight down / across the street
Go straight down the street till you see the hospital then turn left.
Take + road name
Take the third road on the right and you will see the office on the right.

A Unscramble the following sentences.

1. the street / and turn left on Wall Street/ to go straight down/ the quickest way is/.

_____

_____

2. on 5th Avenue / for about 100 meters/ and turn right/ stay on Sunset Boulevard/.

_____

_____

3. the Kmart/ then turn right/till you see/ the Rose Street/ go straight down/.

_____

_____

4. the TaiMall on the right/ on the left/ and you will see/ take the fourth road/.

_____

_____

B Now work with your partners to use the unscrambled sentences to give directions.

Part 4 Practice

Giving directions! Look at the map below, then number the directions in order.

Q: I'm at the museum on 5th St. How do I get to the Italian Restaurant?
A: ☐ It's on the right across from the 7-11.
　 ☐ Turn left and go straight down 5th St.
　 ☐ Go to the corner of 3rd St. and Sunset Blvd.
　 ☐ Turn left on Sunset Blvd. and go past the Mart.

Q: I'm at the McDonald's on 1st St. How do I get to the Post Office?
A: ☐ Turn left on Orange St.
　 ☐ Go past the Zoo and turn right on 4th St.
　 ☐ Turn left and go to the corner of 1st St. and Orange St.
　 ☐ It's on the right.

Q: I'm at the Zoo. How do I get to the Hotel?
A: ☐ Turn right on 5th St.
　 ☐ Go past the Library.
　 ☐ Go two blocks on 5th St. It's on the left across from the Museum.
　 ☐ Turn left and go straight down Orange St.

Part 5 Role Play

A Listen to the CD, then complete the following dialogue 037

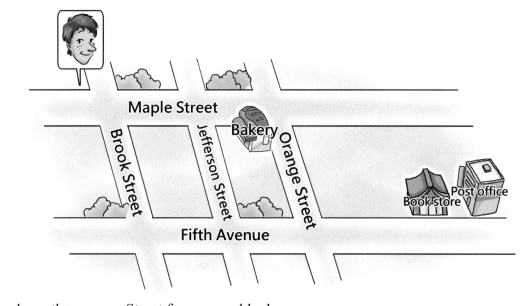

First, go down the _____ Street for _____ blocks.
Then, turn _____ at the _____.
After that, go straight on _____ Street until you get to the _____.
When you get to the _____, turn left.
Then, stay on _____ Avenue for about _____ meters.
It's on your left, next to the _____. You can't miss it!

B Practice the completed dialogue with your partner.

C Use the map to ask and give directions with your partner.

How do I get to the _____ from here?
First, _____.
_____.
_____.
_____.
_____.
_____.

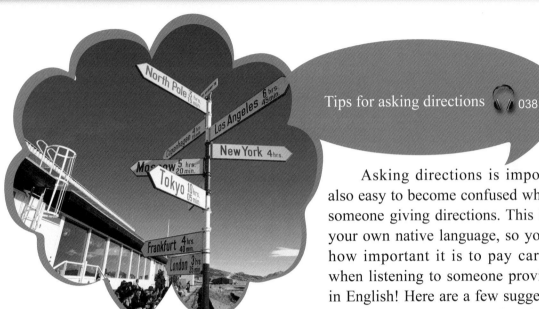

Tips for asking directions 🎧 038

Asking directions is important, but it's also easy to become confused when listening to someone giving directions. This is true even in your own native language, so you can imagine how important it is to pay careful attention when listening to someone provides directions in English! Here are a few suggestions and tips to help you remember the directions as someone gives them to you.

1. Make sure to ask the person giving directions to repeat and / or slow down.
2. In order to help out, repeat each direction the person gives. This will help both you remember the names of streets, turns, etc., as well as help the person giving directions provide clear instructions.
3. Make visual notes while the person describes the route.
4. Once the person has given you directions, repeat the entire set of directions again.

Recognize it! Identify the meanings of the following traffic signs in groups.

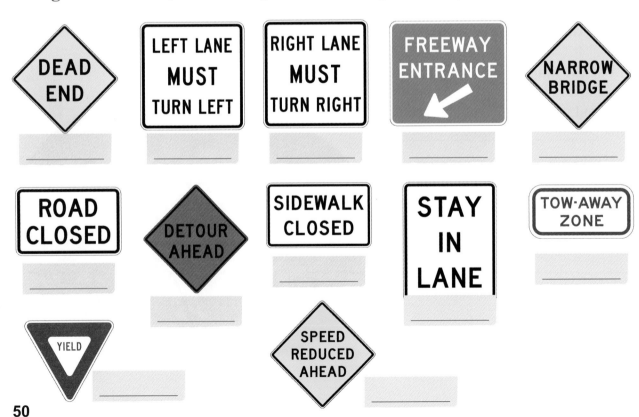

Tips for giving directions 039

1. There are two basic ways to give directions, the "route perspective" characterized by landmarks, and the "survey perspective" characterized by references to cardinal directions (north, south, west, east). The system you use depends on where you are and who you're giving directions to. Most of the time it's best to use a combination.

2. Specify distance. How far along a particular road does the person need to go? There are several different ways to tell them:

   (1) How many blocks or streets they'll pass. For example: "Continue down that street, passing 4 side roads along the way."

   (2) How many traffic lights they'll pass. For example: "You are going to pass three traffic lights before the turn."

   (3) Distance in miles or kilometers. For example: "Go 3 miles on Beverly Road"

   (4) How much time it'll take. For example: "It should be about five minutes on the highway."

   (5) Give them a drop dead point. For example: "If you see the library, you have gone too far."

3. Indicate turns. If it's not a simple, four-way intersection, give a few extra details. Otherwise, tell them to make a left or right. Give them a street name and one landmark (a traffic light, a particular store).

4. Simplify the directions. For example: Turn left onto Baker Street.

5. Say which side of the street their destination is on. For example: "My house is on the left."

Choose it! Match the best answer in the box to each sign.

a. No Parking	b. Advisory Speed	c. Left Turn Only	d. School	e. No Pedestrians
f. Left / Straight Optional Lane	g. Workers	h. No U Turn	i. Railroad Crossing Advance	j. Straight Through Only

Transportation

◆**Language Functions**

Taking a Bus & Taking a Train & Taxi Ride &
Renting a Car

◆**Sentence Patterns**

Usages of How Often, Usages of Present Perfect

◆**Vocabulary in Use**

Renting a car

Part 1 Warm Up

A Listen to these six people and fill in the blanks with what you hear. 040

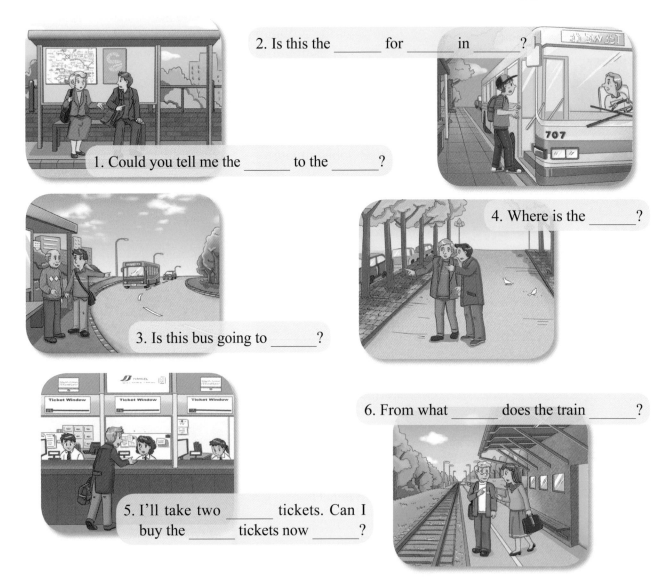

2. Is this the _____ for _____ in _____?

1. Could you tell me the _____ to the _____?

4. Where is the _____?

3. Is this bus going to _____?

6. From what _____ does the train _____?

5. I'll take two _____ tickets. Can I buy the _____ tickets now _____?

B Match each question with its answer.

_____ 1. Which bus goes to the airport?
_____ 2. How often does bus number 102 come?
_____ 3. Could you tell me when the next bus to Central Park will be here?
_____ 4. Could I have a ticket for the next train to Manchester, please?
_____ 5. When does the London train leave, please?
_____ 6. What time does it reach London?

A. The bus comes once an hour.
B. Single or return?
C. You need bus No. 5.
D. 9:25, Platform 3.
E. You should be there at 10:30.
F. It'll be here in ten minutes.

Part 2 Dialogues

1. **Taking a bus** 042

   Daniel: Does this bus go to The British Museum?
Passerby: The British Museum? No, it doesn't.
   Daniel: Which bus will take me there?
Passerby: You need to take the number 7.
   Daniel: Where can I catch it?
Passerby: Right here, at this stop.
   Daniel: Do you happen to know how often a number 7 comes by?
Passerby: About every fifteen or twenty minutes.
   Daniel: Most of the buses I've seen have been pretty crowded. How about the number 7?
Passerby: Yes, I'm afraid it will be, too. It's rush hour now.
   Daniel: Thank you anyway.

Word Bank 041

crowded (adj.) 擁擠的
rush hour (上下班時) 交通擁擠時間

A For each sentence, check ☑ T (true) or F (false)

Daniel is going to The British Museum by taxi.	T ☐	F ☐
A bus number 7 can take Daniel to his destination.	T ☐	F ☐
A bus number 7 comes every fifty minutes.	T ☐	F ☐
Buses are crowded at rush hours.	T ☐	F ☐

B Listen to the dialogue again, and then practice with your partner.

2. Taking a train  044

Jeremy: What time does the next train to Bristol leave?

Railway Station Clerk: At 11:20, from platform 6.

Jeremy: Is it a direct train to Bristol?

Railway Station Clerk: No, you have to change trains at Cardiff.

Jeremy: I see. One ticket to Bristol, please.

Railway Station Clerk: Single or return, sir?

Jeremy: Single, please.

Railway Station Clerk: 45 pounds, please.

Jeremy: Here you are.

Railway Station Clerk: Here's your ticket and change, sir.

Word Bank 043

platform (n.)（鐵路等的）月臺

A For each sentence, check ☑ T (true) or F (false)

Jeremy is going to take a direct train to Bristol. T ☐ F ☐

Jeremy is buying a single ticket to Cardiff. T ☐ F ☐

The single ticket costs Jeremy 45 pounds. T ☐ F ☐

B Listen to the dialogue again, and then practice with your partner.

Part 3 Sentence Patterns *Usages of How often* 045

How often + Auxiliary V. + S. + V.?

How often do you plan to play basketball this summer vacation?
As often as possible. / Every day, if I can.

How often will you visit your mother in San Francisco?
I will try to visit at least once a week

How often did you go to the gymnasium when you were young?
Every weekend, without fail.

How often do you go to the Costco to do your shopping?
Not very often. Perhaps twice a month.

Do you happen to know how often a number 7 comes by?
About every fifteen or twenty minutes.

When you lived in New York, how often did you go to the theater?
We used to go three or four times a year.

A Listen to the following questions and look at the pictures, and then complete each sentence. 046

How often _____?

_____.

How often _____ when he was in San Diego?

_____.

How often _____ from now on?

_____.

B Take turns with your partner to use "How often ..." to ask and answer three questions.

Part 4 Practice

A Bus schedule and route

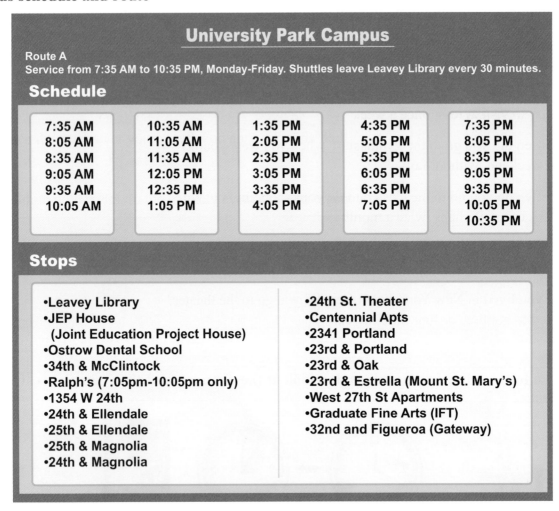

Look at the bus schedule above and answer the following questions.

1. What are the bus service times? _____
2. How often does the bus run? _____
3. How many stops does Route A have? _____

B Complete the exercise with the prepositions in the following box.

at	to	for	by	from	off	on

1. If you want to go _____ bus, you have to go _____ the bus stop.
2. You look _____ the time table.
3. Then you wait _____ your bus.
4. When the bus arrives, you get _____ the bus.
5. You buy a ticket _____ the driver or show your ticket _____ the driver.
6. When you arrive _____ your destination, you get _____ the bus.
7. Sometimes you even have to change buses _____ another bus stop.

Part 5 Role Play

Take a Train! Fill in the blanks and practice the completed dialogue with your
partner.

Clerk

Passenger

👄 Hello. I _____ two tickets to _____ , please, for the _____ p.m. train.

🎧 First or second-class?

👄 What's the _____ in price between the two?

🎧 First class tickets are $ _____ each and second-class tickets are $ _____ .

👄 I'll take two _____ class tickets. Can I buy the return tickets now as well?

🎧 If you like, when would you like to come back?

👄 Is there a train that leaves _____ in the afternoon on Tuesday?

🎧 Yes. There's a train from _____ to _____ leaving daily at 2:00 p.m. Would you like me to book
two tickets for you?

👄 Yes, _____ do. _____ class as well.

Part 1 Warm Up

A Listen to the following talks, then check ☑ what they are talking about. 047

A: Where do you need to go? B: To the Hilton Hotel.	☐ renting a car ☐ riding a taxi
A: How long is the ride? B: It's going to take me about 25 minutes to get there.	☐ renting a car ☐ riding a taxi
A: Fine. How much will this ride be? B: $ 30.	☐ renting a car ☐ riding a taxi
A: Hello, ABC Car Rental. How can I help you? B: Hi, I want to make a reservation.	☐ renting a car ☐ riding a taxi
A: What size car would you like? B: A midsize car please.	☐ renting a car ☐ riding a taxi
A: How many people will be driving the car? B: Just myself.	☐ renting a car ☐ riding a taxi

B When you are taking a taxi or renting a car, what might you say? Check ☑ the correct answers.

☐ Your destination is just ahead.

☐ How much would it be to Holiday Inn?

☐ Take me to Holiday Inn, please.

☐ Would you put my baggage in the trunk?

☐ I'd like to rent a car, please.

☐ Full-size, please. What's the rate?

☐ I'd like to have insurance just in case.

☐ What type of car would you like?

Part 2 Dialogues

1. **Riding in a taxi** 049

Sam: Could you take me to the Hyatt Hotel, please? How long do you think it will take to get there?

Taxi driver: It's very close to the airport, so it should take about 15 minutes to get there.

Sam: That's perfect, because I had a really long flight.

Taxi driver: Where are you travelling from?

Sam: Taipei, Taiwan.

Taxi driver: Here we are. We have arrived.

Sam: Great! How much will that be?

Taxi driver: Your fare is 8 dollars.

Sam: Here's a 10. Please, keep the change.

Taxi driver: Thank you. Have a good stay!

Sam: Thank you.

Word Bank 048

close to (phr.) 接近於；靠近
perfect (adj.) 完美的；理想的
keep the change (phr.) 不用找零錢

A For each sentence, check ☑ T (true) or F (false)

The Hyatt Hotel is far away from the airport.	T ☐	F ☐
It will take the taxi driver fifty minutes to drive from the airport to the Hyatt Hotel.	T ☐	F ☐
Sam must be tired because of a long flight.	T ☐	F ☐
Sam will take his change back.	T ☐	F ☐

B Listen to the dialogue again, and then practice with your partner.

2. Renting a car  🎧 051

Rent-A-Car Clerk: Good morning. May I help you?

Kobe: I'd like to rent a car, please.

Rent-A-Car Clerk: Okay. Full-size, mid-size or compact, sir?

Kobe: Compact, please. What's the rate?

Rent-A-Car Clerk: 50 dollars a day with unlimited mileage.

Kobe: And I'd like to have insurance just in case.

Rent-A-Car Clerk: Is there an additional driver?

Kobe: No.

Rent-A-Car Clerk: If you want full coverage insurance, it will be 7 dollars per day. It includes collision damage waiver and personal accident insurance.

Kobe: All right. I'll take it.

Rent-A-Car Clerk: Here is our brochure, sir. Err... compact... OK. Please choose a model in this section.

Kobe: How about this one?

Rent-A-Car Clerk: All right. How many days would you like to use it?

Kobe: Five days.

Rent-A-Car Clerk: May I see your driver's license and credit card, please?

Kobe: Is the international driving license fine?

Rent-A-Car Clerk: Yes, it is. Thank you. Please fill in this form. Can you check this box, and put your initials here, and again here.

Word Bank 🎧 050

compact car (n.) 小型汽車
rate (n.) 費用
unlimited (adj.) 無限制的
mileage (n.) 總英里數
in case (phr.) 以防萬一
additional (adj.) 額外的
full coverage insurance (n.) 全險
collision (n.) 碰撞；相撞
damage (n.) 損害；損失
waiver (n.) 放棄；棄權證書
accident (n.) 意外
section (n.) (事物的) 部分
driver's license (n.) 駕駛執照
initials (n.) 姓名的首字母

A For each sentence, check ☑ T (true) or F (false)

Kobe is renting a full-size car.	T ☐	F ☐
The full coverage insurance includes collision damage waiver and personal accident insurance.	T ☐	F ☐
Kobe will rent a car for five days.	T ☐	F ☐
Kobe has to pay totally 285 dollars for renting a car for five days.	T ☐	F ☐

B Listen to the dialogue again, and then practice with your partner.

Part 3 Sentence Patterns *Usages of Present Perfect* 052

Positive Present Perfect   S. + has/ have + V. (p.p.)

We have arrived.	I have seen that movie twenty times.
She has been in England for six months.	I have met him once before.

Negative Present Perfect   S. + has/ have not + V. (p.p.)

We have not slept all night.	He has not seen the new film.
I have not eaten breakfast today.	You have not been to Asia.

To make a question, put "have" or "has" in front of the subject

Have you read the book yet?	Where have I left my umbrella?
Why has he gone already?	What have you done today?

A Make the positive present perfect sentences.

We / read / that book

_____

He / live / here for three years

_____

You / know / David for ten years

_____

B Make the negative present perfect sentences.

She / not / see / "The Lord of the Rings"

_____

You / not / study / French for ten years

_____

They / not / arrive / yet

_____

63

C Make present perfect "yes / no" or "wh" questions

They / go / to the USA?

You / go / to Australia?

Where / you / be?

Part 4 Practice

Taking a taxi! Complete the dialogue by using the sentences listed in the box.

• This is it.	• How much is it?	• How long will it take to get there
• The traffic is quite heavy.	• Here you go.	• Where are you headed
• How much do you think it will cost?		

Sabrina: Hey taxi!

Taxi Driver: _____, Madam?

Sabrina: I'm going to the Metropolitan Museum. Could you take me there?

Taxi Driver: Sure. I can.

Sabrina: _____?

Taxi Driver: _____, so it may take a while.

Sabrina: _____

Taxi Driver: It will probably be about $30.

Sabrina: Okay.

        (After 25 minutes)

Taxi Driver: _____

Sabrina: _____

Taxi Driver: That will be $28.

Sabrina: _____

Taxi Driver: Thank you! Have a nice day.

Sabrina: You're welcome. Have a good one, too.

Part 5 Role Play

Rent a car! Fill in the blanks and practice the completed dialogue with your partner.

Clerk   Tourist

I want to rent a _____ car for _____ days, please.

Our rate is $ _____ with _____.

That's fine.

Can I have your _____, credit card and _____, please.

Here _____.

And _____ here in town?

I'm staying at the _____.

Would you like the _____ with that? It's eight dollars a day.

Yes.

Sign here, _____.

Do you have a _____?

There is already one in the car.

Good.

Here are _____. Have a nice trip.

Thank you.

Tips on riding a bus 🎧 053

1. Find out if you can get a free or discounted pass for buses by reason of age, youth, student status, or disability, etc.
2. Find out if it would be economical to get a pass or multi-trip ticket for your regular journeys.

3. When the bus arrives, check the destination sign and route number on the bus to make sure it is the bus you want.
4. Remember that in some countries, the seats in front are reserved by law for handicapped riders, or elderly people.

Sentence Completion

( ) 1. I'd like to buy a _____ ticket to London please. I'm leaving today and coming back next Monday.
    (A) go-and-come-back   (B) there-and-back
    (C) return   (D) two-way

( ) 2. I'm here to meet my friends on the 12:15 train from Edinburgh. Can you tell me if the train left Edinburgh _____?
    (A) on time   (B) at time   (C) in time   (D) of time

( ) 3. Our train is leaving from _____ 14 at 10 o'clock.
    (A) track   (B) stand   (C) place   (D) platform

( ) 4. We are sorry to have to announce that the Leeds train that was due to arrive at 12:20 _____ by one hour and will now arrive at 13:20.
    (A) delays   (B) delayed   (C) is late   (D) has been delayed

( ) 5. Rose was hungry on the train journey from Leeds to Manchester so she went to the _____ to get something to eat.
    (A) café   (B) restaurant   (C) dining room   (D) buffet car

Tips on renting a car 🎧 054

1. Check the rental car companies' Web sites directly to see whether you can get a cheaper rate there.
2. Don't forget to fill the tank back up before you return the car. If you fail to do so, expect to pay much more than the market price for the gasoline you owe.

3. If you return your car late, the rental agency may charge you as much as a full day's rental, sometimes at a rate higher than before. If you are going to be late, call the agency and explain your situation. It may help.

Sentence Completion

( ) 1. Another word for a taxi is a _____.
   (A) comber   (B) concierge   (C) cab   (D) consultant
( ) 2. A taxi _____, often found outside of an airport or train station, is an area on a street where taxis line up and wait for passengers.
   (A) circus   (B) charade   (C) stand   (D) segment
( ) 3. Taxi drivers drive people to various destinations and the _____ can vary depending on the distance and length of a trip.
   (A) faxes   (B) tags   (C) tariffs   (D) fares
( ) 4. Taxi drivers _____ up passengers throughout their shifts.
   (A) lift   (B) pick   (C) carry   (D) snatch
( ) 5. People often give taxi drivers extra money (in addition to the fares) known as _____.
   (A) tips   (B) taxes   (C) tariffs   (D) tolls

Hotel

◆**Language Functions**

Reserving a Room & Requesting and Complaining

◆**Sentence Patterns**

Usages of Would like, Expressions of Complaints

◆**Vocabulary in Use**

Hotel Room Services

Reserving a Room

Part 1 Warm Up

A Listen to the following dialogue and fill in the missing words in the blanks. 🎧 055

> Client: Hi, good morning. I'd like to _____ a reservation for the _____ weekend in _____. Do you have any vacancies?
>
> Receptionist: Yes sir, we have _____ rooms available for that particular weekend. And what is the exact _____ of your arrival?
>
> Client: The _____.
>
> Receptionist: How _____ will you be staying?
>
> Client: I'll be staying for _____ nights.
>
> Receptionist: How many _____ is the reservation for?
>
> Client: There will be _____ of us.
>
> Receptionist: And would you like a room with twin beds or a _____ bed?
>
> Client: A double bed, please.
>
> Receptionist: Great. And would you prefer to have a room with a view of the _____?
>
> Client: If that _____ of room is available, I would love to have an ocean view. What's the rate for the room?
>
> Receptionist: Your room is five _____ and _____ dollars per night.

B What kind of services most hotels usually offer? Check ☑ the correct answers.

☐ Bar and restaurant	☐ Shopping and entertainment	☐ Laundry Services
☐ Arts and sightseeing	☐ Concierge Services	☐ Fitness and sauna
☐ Parking services	☐ Internet service	☐ Transfers from International Airport

Part 2 Dialogues

1. Reserving a room. 057

Receptionist: Good morning, Francisco Bay Inn. May I help you?

Mrs. Brown: Yes. I'd like to book a double room with a sea view for May 12th and 13th, please.

Receptionist: Certainly, madam. I'll just check what we have available... Yes, we have a room on the 7th floor with a really splendid view.

Mrs. Brown: Fine. How much is the charge per night?

Receptionist: It's $120 per night.

Mrs. Brown: That's fine.

Receptionist: Who's the booking for, please, madam?

Mrs. Brown: Mr. and Mrs. Brown, that's B-R-O-W-N.

Receptionist: Okay, let me make sure I got that: Mr. and Mrs. Brown. Double room for May 12th and 13th. Is that correct?

Mrs. Brown: Yes it is. Thank you.

Receptionist: Let me give you your confirmation number. It's: 8687573. I'll repeat that: 8687573. Thank you for choosing Francisco Bay Inn and have a nice day. Goodbye.

Mrs. Brown: Goodbye.

Word Bank 056

available (adj.) 有空的；可用的
splendid (adj.) 壯麗的
view (n.) 景色
charge (n.) 費用
per (prep.) 每

A For each sentence, check ☑ T (true) or F (false)

Mrs. Brown is booking a room at San Francisco Hotel.	T ☐	F ☐
Mrs. Brown would like a double room with a mountain view.	T ☐	F ☐
The room that Mrs. Brown will stay is on eighth floor.	T ☐	F ☐

B Listen to the dialogue again, and then practice with your partner.

2. Checking in 059

Receptionist: Good evening. May I help you?

Albert: Yes, I have a reservation. The name is Albert Chen.

Receptionist: Mr. Chen... Ah, yes. Would you fill out this form, please?

Albert: Sure... Here you are.

Receptionist: You've booked a single room for 3 nights, is that right?

Albert: Yes... and I want a non-smoking room, please.

Receptionist: Sure, no problem. Your room is on the 5th floor, Room 512. Here's your key.

Albert: Thanks. By the way, is there a safe deposit box in my room?

Receptionist: Yes, it's inside the closet.

Albert: Great!

Word Bank 058

fill out (phr.) 填寫
form (n.) 表格
safe deposit box (n.) 貴重物品保管箱
closet (n.) 衣櫥

A Answer the following questions based on the dialogue above.

1. What is Albert doing?
2. What kind of room has Albert booked?
3. How many nights will Albert stay at the hotel?
4. What is a safe deposit box for?

B Listen to the dialogue again, and then practice with your partner.

Part 3 Sentence Patterns *Reserving a hotel room* 060

Customer:

Do you have any vacancies / a room available for tonight?

I'd like to make a reservation for two nights starting May 10.

I'd like a single room/ double room/twin room with two separate beds/ room with two single beds, please.

I'll be staying / I am going to stay for two nights.

I am going to need the room until August 7th.

I want a room with a nice sea view.

What is the room rate for a single room per night?

Hotel Receptionist:

I'll check to see if there are any vacancies. Please hold on.

I'm sorry, but we are fully booked/ all booked up.

Sorry, we are full tonight/ at the moment.

How many rooms will you need/ would you like to reserve?

What kind/type of room would you like to have/ do you have in mind?

How long will you be staying here? /How many days would you like the room for?

The hotel charges 40 dollars for an overnight stay.

A Work with your partner to use these sentence patterns to reserve a hotel room.

_____

_____

_____

_____

Part 4 Practice

Surf the Internet! Booking rooms in a hotel

You and your family are taking a trip to a foreign country and plan to stay in a hotel for three nights. You are in charge of booking rooms for them using the Internet. Fill in the following information according to what you find on the Internet in regard to which hotel you plan to stay at.

Hotel Information

Name of Hotel: _____

Mailing address: _____

Telephone number: _____

Room types available: _____

Bed types available: _____

Reservation Information

Date of check-in: _____

Date of check-out: _____

Number of rooms you book: _____

Bed type and /or Room type(s): _____

Rate per Room per Night: _____

Taxes: _____

Room features (description):

_____

_____

_____

_____

Part 5 Role Play

Pair work! Fill in the blanks and practice the completed dialogue with your partner.

Receptionist   Guest

🙎 Good _____, _____. May I help you?

🙎 Do you have a room _____?

🙎 Yes, what kind of room would you like?

🙎 There are _____ of us. We'd like _____.

🙎 For _____?

🙎 _____ nights.

🙎 Will that be smoking or _____?

🙎 _____, please. What's the _____?

🙎 $_____ per night.

🙎 That'll be fine.

🙎 How will you _____, sir?

🙎 Here's my Visa Card.

🙎 Thank you, _____. Here's the key card for room _____. Have a nice day.

Requesting and Complaining

Part 1 Warm Up

A Listen to following dialogues and check ☑ with the customer in each dialogue is doing.

🎧 061

I would like extra soap and shampoo left in the room.
I'll attend to that immediately.
☐ making a complaint
☐ making a request

The sink is leaking in the bathroom.
Sorry for the inconvenience, maintenance will be by shorty to fix the problem.
☐ making a complaint
☐ making a request

We ran out of toilet paper. Is it possible to get more?
Of course, ma'am. I'll send more up immediately.
☐ making a complaint
☐ making a request

I specifically requested an ocean view, but the room I was given has a view of the pool.
I'm sorry about the mix-up sir, we'll change your room immediately.
☐ making a complaint
☐ making a request

B What might you say while requesting or complaining to hotel services? Check ☑ the correct answers.

☐ Can I get a wake-up call at 7:30 AM?
☐ Our bed sheets are dirty. Could you please change them?
☐ How much does it cost to make a call to Taiwan?
☐ The coffee-maker doesn't work.
☐ Is breakfast included in the price?

Part 2 **Dialogues**

1. **Requesting room service.** 063

Clerk: Front desk. May I help you?

Keiko: Yes. This is Room 5512. May I have some extra towels, please?

Clerk: Sure. I'll send some up right away.

Keiko: Oh, and could I borrow an iron?

Clerk: Certainly. I'll send one up with the towels.

Keiko: Great! Oh, I'd like a wake-up call tomorrow morning, please.

Clerk: Certainly. What time would you like us to call you?

Keiko: Umm... 7:30 a.m. would be fine.

Clerk: Sure.

Keiko: Thanks a lot.

Clerk: You're welcome.

Word Bank 062

front desk (n.) 櫃檯
extra (adj.) 額外的
towel (n.) 毛巾
iron (n.) 熨斗

A Answer the following questions based on the dialogue above.

1. What is Keiko requesting the clerk to send up to her room?
2. What time does Keiko want to get up tomorrow morning?

B Listen to the dialogue again, and then practice with your partner.

2. Complaining about the room.  065

Albert: Excuse me, I am staying at Room 512. My room faces the main street and it's very noisy. Also, there doesn't seem to be heat in my room. Could you change my room?

Receptionist: Umm... Let me check to see if there are any vacant rooms... Ah, I can let you have Room 588. It's facing the garden so it should be a lot quieter.

Albert: Oh, fantastic! I hope there's heat in this room!

Receptionist: I'm sure there is, but if there's any problem, please let me know.

Albert: Thanks a lot for your help.

Receptionist: You're welcome. Enjoy your stay.

Word Bank 064

face (v.) 面對
noisy (adj.) 吵雜的
heat (n.) 暖氣
vacant (adj.) 空著的
fantastic (adj.) 極好的

A Answer the following questions based on the dialogue above.

1. What are the problems with the Room 512 that Albert is staying?
2. What is the receptionist going to do with Albert's complaints?

B Listen to the dialogue again, and then practice with your partner.

Part 3 Sentence Patterns *Expressions of Complaints* 066

The room is very dirty.
The TV is out of order.
The TV in my room doesn't seem to work.
The toilet in my room doesn't flush.
The air-conditioner in my room isn't cold enough.
The tap in the bathroom is dripping.
The faucet in the bathroom is leaking.
My room faces the main street and it's very noisy.

A Use the sentence patterns above to complete the following sentences.

1. The room is _____ .

2. _____ is out of order.

3. _____ in my room doesn't seem to work.

4. _____ in my room doesn't/isn't _____ .

5. _____ in the bathroom is _____ .

6. My room faces _____ and it's _____ .

B Work with your partner to make complaints to bad hotel services.

_____

_____

_____

_____

Part 4 Practice

Group work! Six students take turns to be the receptionist at the front desk of a hotel and guests. The receptionist asks the guests the following questions, and then writes down their answers in the table below:

1. How may I help you?
2. Can I have your name, please?
3. How do you spell that?
4. Would you like a single or a double room?
5. How many people are you traveling with?
6. How many nights will you be staying?
7. Would you like a wake-up call?
8. How will you be paying?

Name	Room Type	Number of People	Number of Nights	Wake-up Call (Y/N)	Method of Payment

Part 5 Role Play

Pair Work! Fill in the blanks and practice the completed dialog with your partner.

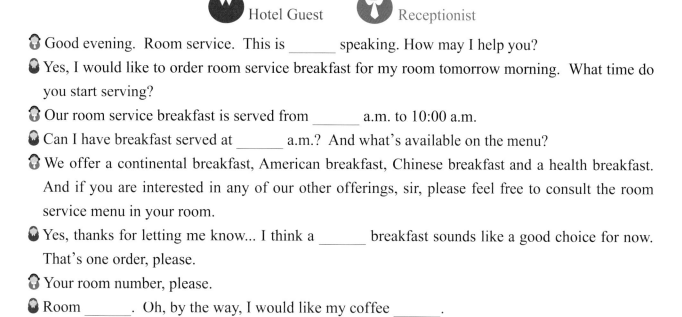

Hotel Guest   Receptionist

🎧 Good evening. Room service. This is _____ speaking. How may I help you?

👤 Yes, I would like to order room service breakfast for my room tomorrow morning. What time do you start serving?

🎧 Our room service breakfast is served from _____ a.m. to 10:00 a.m.

👤 Can I have breakfast served at _____ a.m.? And what's available on the menu?

🎧 We offer a continental breakfast, American breakfast, Chinese breakfast and a health breakfast. And if you are interested in any of our other offerings, sir, please feel free to consult the room service menu in your room.

👤 Yes, thanks for letting me know... I think a _____ breakfast sounds like a good choice for now. That's one order, please.

🎧 Your room number, please.

👤 Room _____. Oh, by the way, I would like my coffee _____.

🎧 All right, sir. We will send one order of our _____ breakfast to your room at _____ tomorrow morning to room _____.

👤 Thank you very much.

Hotel Booking 🎧 067

Many trips and hotel bookings are now purchased through commercial websites such as Expedia.com, Travelocity.com, Orbitz.com, and Hotels.com. Be sure to shop around sites for the best deal and don't forget to visit the hotel website itself. Individual hotel websites often have deals that don't appear on commercial sites. And be sure to read reviews of the hotel on these commercial booking sites.

A Match the hotel symbols with the words in the box.

| air conditioned | bar or lounge | gym | 24 hour room service | web access |
| satellite TV | wheelchair access | gift and book shop | laundry service | money exchange |

_____   _____   _____   _____   _____

_____   _____   _____   _____   _____

B Match the correct questions from the box into each reply.

1. What is the star designation of your hotel?
2. What is the easiest way to book a room at your hotel?
3. How long does it take to get from the international airport to your hotel?
4. Can I leave my baggage at the hotel?
5. Is your hotel located near the downtown area, or it is more residential?
6. When is breakfast served?

Guest: _____
Front Desk: We are conveniently situated between the business and entertainment district.
Guest: _____
Front Desk: It only takes 20 minutes to get from the airport to our hotel.
Guest: _____
Front Desk: We are a four-star hotel.
Guest: _____
Front Desk: Using our online booking system.
Guest: _____
Front Desk: There is a baggage room where you can leave your bags if you plan to arrive early or leave late.
Guest: _____
Front Desk: Breakfast is served 6:30-10:00 a.m. on weekdays, and 7:00-11:00 a.m. on weekends
and on public holidays.

Room Service 🎧 068
Room service usually provides the ultimate in convenience: all kinds of drinks and hospitable food, from snacks to full course meals. The room service menu changes with the seasons, but guests can always find an up-to-date menu in their room. The menu offerings are available 24-hours a day.

A Match the pictures with the words in the box.

toothbrush	comb	shower cap	towel	pillow
shaver	soap	hair dryer	blanket	garment hanger

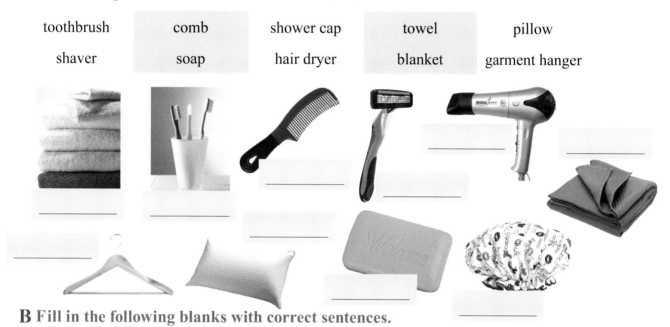

B Fill in the following blanks with correct sentences.

1. What's the 10 dollars for?
2. Thank you. Goodbye.
3. Can I pay with traveler's checks?
4. Yes, I'd like to check out now. My name's Jason, room 702. Here's the key.
5. Here you are.
6. Sure.

Receptionist: Good morning. May I help you?
Jason: _____

Receptionist: One moment, please, sir. ... Here's your bill. Would you like to check and see if the amount is correct?
Jason: _____

Receptionist: That's for the phone calls you made from your room.
Jason: _____

Receptionist: Certainly. May I have your passport, please?
Jason: _____

Receptionist: Could you sign each check here for me?
Jason: _____

Receptionist: Here are your receipt and your change, sir. Thank you.
Jason: _____

Tourism English

Restaurant

◆Language Functions

Reserving a Table and Ordering & Complaining

◆Sentence Patterns

Expressions of Placing Order, Expressions of Complaints

◆Vocabulary in Use

Table items & food

Reserving a Table and Ordering

Part 1 Warm Up

Check it! When you order food in an English speaking country, you may see the following food items on menus. Check ☑ what they belong to.

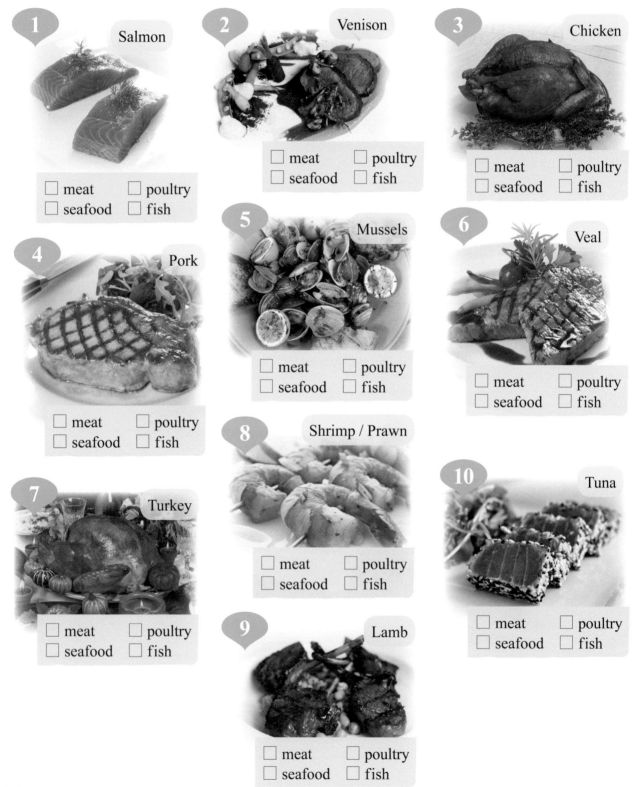

1 Salmon
- [ ] meat
- [ ] poultry
- [ ] seafood
- [ ] fish

2 Venison
- [ ] meat
- [ ] poultry
- [ ] seafood
- [ ] fish

3 Chicken
- [ ] meat
- [ ] poultry
- [ ] seafood
- [ ] fish

4 Pork
- [ ] meat
- [ ] poultry
- [ ] seafood
- [ ] fish

5 Mussels
- [ ] meat
- [ ] poultry
- [ ] seafood
- [ ] fish

6 Veal
- [ ] meat
- [ ] poultry
- [ ] seafood
- [ ] fish

7 Turkey
- [ ] meat
- [ ] poultry
- [ ] seafood
- [ ] fish

8 Shrimp / Prawn
- [ ] meat
- [ ] poultry
- [ ] seafood
- [ ] fish

9 Lamb
- [ ] meat
- [ ] poultry
- [ ] seafood
- [ ] fish

10 Tuna
- [ ] meat
- [ ] poultry
- [ ] seafood
- [ ] fish

Part 2 Dialogues

1. Reserving a Table 070

Receptionist: Hello. You've called the Golden Coin Restaurant. What can I do for you?

Customer: Oh, hello. I would like to book a table for tomorrow evening. Are there any tables available?

Receptionist: Just a moment, sir. Let me check the bookings. You are lucky. We have some available tables for tomorrow evening.

Customer: OK. That's good.

Receptionist: For how many people should the reservation be?

Customer: I would like a table for six, please.

Receptionist: Do you have any preferences?

Customer: Er..., I would prefer it to be by the window, if that's possible.

Receptionist: All right. So, you want a table for six, by the window, for tomorrow evening.

Customer: Yes, that is correct.

Receptionist: And the reservation will be for... What is your name?

Customer: Oh, yes. My name is Justin Bieber.

Receptionist: OK, sir. I have taken that down.

Customer: Thank you very much.

Receptionist: Goodbye.

Word Bank 069

booking (n.) 預訂
preference (n.) 偏愛
take down (phr.) 寫下

A For each sentence, check ☑ T (true) or F (false)

The customer is calling for reserving a table at a restaurant.	T ☐	F ☐
The Golden Coin Restaurant has only one table available for tomorrow evening.	T ☐	F ☐
The customer prefers a table by the window.	T ☐	F ☐

B Listen to the dialogue again, and then practice with your partner.

Tourism English

2. Ordering 072

Waiter: Are you ready to order, sir?

Mr. Brown: Yes. I'll have the corn & spicy chicken chowder for starters and my wife would like pumpkin stew.

Waiter: One corn & spicy chicken chowder and one pumpkin stew. What would you like for the main course?

Mr. Brown: I'll have the Bourbon steak and my wife would like the Salmon steak with cream sauce.

Waiter: I'm afraid the salmon is off.

Mrs. Brown: Oh dear. Er... What else do you recommend?

Waiter: The trout is very good.

Mrs. Brown: OK. I'll have that. Do you have any Greek salad?

Waiter: No, I'm sorry, we don't.

Mrs. Brown: Just give me a Caesar salad then.

Mr. Brown: Same for me.

Waiter: Certainly. Would you like something to drink?

Mr. Brown: Yes, please. May I see the wine list?

Waiter: Certainly. Here you are.

Mr. Brown: A bottle of Chablis 99, please.

Waiter: Excellent choice!

Word Bank 071

spicy (adj.) 加有香料的；辛辣的
chowder (n.) 海鮮雜燴濃湯
starter (n.) 開胃菜
pumpkin (n.) 南瓜
stew (n.) 燉煮的食物
main course (n.) 主菜
steak (n.) 牛排；肉排；魚排
salmon (n.) 鮭魚
sauce (n.) 調味醬，醬汁
recommend (v.) 推薦
salad (n.) 沙拉
wine list (n.) 酒類一覽表
excellent (adj.) 出色的；傑出的
choice(n.) 選擇

A For each sentence, check ☑ T (true) or F (false)

Mr. Brown is ordering the corn & spicy chicken chowder for his main course.	T ☐	F ☐
The Salmon steak is sold out at this restaurant.	T ☐	F ☐
Both Mr. and Mrs. Brown are ordering Greek salad.	T ☐	F ☐

B Listen to the dialogue again, and then practice with your partner.

Part 3 **Sentence Patterns**   *Expressions of Placing Order* 073

For starters I'll have the soup and for the main course I'd like the roast beef.
Could I have chips instead of baked potatoes, please?
What is the house special today?
Is there anything you would recommend?
Could I see the wine menu, please?
I'll have a glass of white wine, please.
Which wine would you recommend?

A Look at the following menu and take turns with your partner to play the roles of waiter and customer.

· MENU ·

SEASIDE STARTERS

Jumbo Coconut Shrimp $ 8.25   Buffalo Chicken Wings $8.75   Crab Cakes $9.50

Lobster Nachos $9.75   BBQ Scallops $9.25   Steamed Clams $10.99

STEAK & CHICKEN

Center-Cut NY Strip Steak $ 21.99   Maple-Glazed Chicken $12.75

SOUPS & SALADS

Clam Chowder $4.99   Creamy Potato Bacon Soup $5.50
Caesar Salad with shrimp $ 10.50   Caesar Salad with chicken $9.50

BEER

Bottled Beer   Draft Beer

Heineken   Bud Lite   Miller Lite   Budwiser   Sam Adams   Bud Light

Waiter: May I take your order now?
Customer: Yes. For starter I'll have _____ and for the main course I'd like _____
Customer: Is there anything you would recommend?
Waiter: Yes. The _____ is very good.
Customer: OK. I'll have _____ and a bottle/ glass of _____.

B Now work with your partners to use these sentence patterns to order food.

Part 4 Practice

Having Meals in a Restaurant!

You are visiting a foreign country. One of the first things you would like to do is try the local cuisine. Fill in the following information according to what you find on the Internet in regard to which restaurant you choose.

Restaurant Information
Name of restaurant: _____

Mailing address: _____

Telephone number: _____

Lunch hours: _____

Dinner hours: _____

What you plan to eat
Lunch
Appetizer: _____

Soup: _____

Main course: _____

Dessert: _____

Beverage: _____

Total lunch bill: _____

Tip you will leave for the waiter/waitress: _____

Dinner
Appetizer: _____

Soup: _____

Main course: _____

Dessert: _____

Beverage: _____

Total dinner bill: _____

Part 5 Role Play

Group Work! Fill in the blanks and practice the completed dialogue with your partners.

Waiter　　　Customer 1　　　Customer 2

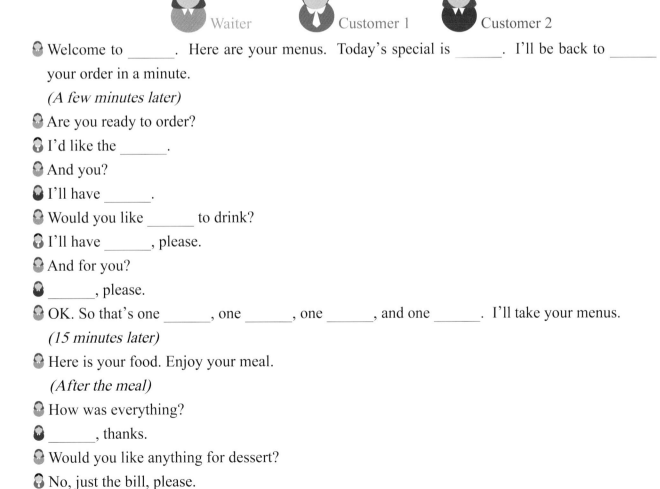

Welcome to _____. Here are your menus. Today's special is _____. I'll be back to _____ your order in a minute.

(A few minutes later)

Are you ready to order?

I'd like the _____.

And you?

I'll have _____.

Would you like _____ to drink?

I'll have _____, please.

And for you?

_____, please.

OK. So that's one _____, one _____, one _____, and one _____. I'll take your menus.

(15 minutes later)

Here is your food. Enjoy your meal.

(After the meal)

How was everything?

_____, thanks.

Would you like anything for dessert?

No, just the bill, please.

Part 1 Warm Up

What may customers say while complaining about the meal they ordered at a restaurant? Check ☑ the correct answers.

☐ This wine tastes like vinegar.

☐ This coffee is stone cold.

☐ I'm very sorry, madam, I'll bring you another bottle.

☐ This soup tastes too salty.

☐ The service here is very slow. I ordered my meal more than an hour ago!

☐ This steak is undercooked. It's rare, and I asked for a well-done steak.

Part 2 Dialogues

1.**Complaining about the bad taste of meals.** 075

Venus: Oh, here comes our food!

Albert: Finally!

Waiter: Here's your salmon, and here's your steak.

Albert: OK! Let's eat! Oh! My fish isn't fresh! I can't eat it! How's your steak?

Venus: It's tough and dry. It tastes like a piece of leather! Excuse me!
(Calling the waiter)

Venus: We can't eat this food. His fish isn't fresh, and my steak is tough and dry.

Waiter: I'm sorry. I'll take it back to the kitchen.

Word Bank 074

tough (adj.) 咬不動的
taste (v.) 嚐起來
leather (n.) 皮革

A **For each sentence, check ✓ T (true) or F (false)**

Albert and Venus have a long wait for their dishes.	T ☐	F ☐
Albert's fish is very fresh.	T ☐	F ☐
Venus' steak is touch and dry.	T ☐	F ☐
The waiter is going to change dishes for Albert and Venus.	T ☐	F ☐

B **Listen to the dialogue again, and then practice with your partner.**

2. Complaining about the delay of meals. 077

Helen: Excuse me, I've been waiting for over 30 minutes and my meal still hasn't come.

Waiter: What did you order?

Helen: Steak and salad.

Waiter: Just one moment, I'll go and see what the delay is.

Helen: Thank you.
(After a few minutes)

Waiter: Sorry to keep you waiting. Here's your steak and salad.

Helen: Thank you. Sorry, but this knife is a little dirty. Could you bring me another one?

Waiter: I'm very sorry. Yes, of course.
(After a moment)

Waiter: Here you are, a new knife and fork.

Helen: Thanks. I'm afraid the music is a little too loud. Can you turn it down?

Waiter: I'll see what I can do. Is there anything else?

Helen: Actually, there is. I ordered my steak medium. This is well-done. I'd like another one, please.

Word Bank 076

meal (n.) 膳食；一餐
knife (n.) 刀
fork (n.) 叉
loud (adj.) 大聲的
actually (adv.) 實際上
medium (adj.) 中等熟度的
well-done (adj.) 完全煮熟的

A For each sentence, check ☑ T (true) or F (false)

	T	F
Helen has been waiting for her meal for 30 minutes.	☐	☐
Helen asks the waiter to turn on the music.	☐	☐
Helen ordered a well-done steak.	☐	☐

B Listen to the dialogue again, and then practice with your partner.

Part 3 Sentence Patterns *Expressions of Complaints* 078

When will our table be ready? We've been here for over 25 minutes.
We've been waiting for our food for over 25 minutes.
Excuse me, this soup is cold.
There is a fly in my soup!
I can't eat this. It's too salty.
This steak is too tough.
This steak is rare. I want it well-done.
This fish is not fresh.
I ordered baked potato, not French fries.
There's something wrong with our bill. We didn't order any desserts.
May I speak with your manager, please?

A Take turns with your partner to play the roles of waiter and customer in the following three dialogues.

Customer: Waiter, this is not what I ordered.
   Waiter: I'm sorry, what did you order?
Customer: I ordered _____, but this is _____.
   Waiter: I understand, I'll change right away.

Customer: Waiter, I've been here for _____ already. How come my order is not here yet? What is taking so long?
   Waiter: I'm sorry, I'll go check on it immediately.

   Waiter: What's wrong, sir? Is there anything I can help you with?
Customer: Well, as you can see, I ordered a _____ and the _____ is _____.
   Waiter: I really apologize for this mistake. Allow me to get you a better dish.

B Now work with your partners to use these sentence patterns to make complaints.

_____

_____

_____

Part 4 Practice

Complaint Letter! Complaint on the food preparation at a restaurant.

Read the following complaint letter and use your own words to replace the words underlined in the letter.

Julia Roberts
2054 Maple Street
Monterey Park, CA 91754

12 May 2013

Mr. Brad Pitt
Golden Coin Restaurant
1190 Sunset Boulevard
Monterey Park, CA 91754

Dear Mr. Pitt,

I am Julia, writing to you to inform you that the services given at your restaurant were not satisfied. On the 8 May night, I went to your restaurant with my family to celebrate my son's birthday. Unfortunately, what I am not satisfied is about the several lacking regarding the preparation of the food.

Firstly, we reached there and found the table was not clean although there were some of your workers there. After 15 minutes waiting to make orders, a waiter came to us with an annoying face. After making orders, we had to wait for almost 20 minutes for our food being served. On that time, there were only 5 tables of customers. Surprisingly, there was a hair in my pork chop and also a fly in my husband's corn soup. Besides that, the food served was not delicious.

Therefore, I am writing this to ask you to please make sure your food preparation is clean. Please ask your workers to give the best services to customers in order to ensure the customers satisfied with the services at your restaurant. As a well-known restaurant in this city, you have to take serious in these matters.

I'm looking forward to receiving your explanation of these matters. Thank you.

Yours faithfully,

Julia Roberts

Dear _____,

I am _____, writing to you to inform you that the services given at your restaurant were not satisfied. On _____ _____ night, I went to your restaurant with _____ to _____. Unfortunately, what I am not satisfied is about the several lacking regarding _____.

Firstly, we reached there and found _____ although there were some of your workers there. After _____ waiting to make orders, a waiter came to us _____. After making orders, we had to wait for _____ for our food being served. On that time, there were only _____ _____. Surprisingly, there was _____ and also _____. Besides that, the food served _____.

Therefore, I am writing this to ask you to please make sure _____. Please ask your workers to _____ in order to ensure the customers satisfied with the services at your restaurant. As a well-known restaurant in this city, you have to _____.

I'm looking forward to receiving your explanation of these matters. Thank you.

Yours faithfully,

_____

Part 5 Role Play

Just do it! Write the following twelve sentences on twelve pieces of paper or cards. Students take it in turn to pick up a piece of paper or card. They must communicate the complaint on the card by replacing the underlined words.

These _____ are very _____.

There is a ___ in my ____.

The _____ has _____ all over my _____.

You said this _____ was __ _____ but it's very _____.

A _____ just _____ under the table and bit my finger.

These _____ are too _____.

These _____ _____ are _____.

I asked for a _____ beer but this one is _____.

I asked for a _____ but this one is _____.

You have put _____ on the _____ but we didn't _ _____ any.

I asked for a ____ without any _____ but this one has ___ in it.

I asked for a _____ without any _____ but this one has ___ in it.

This dish has _____ in it and I'm _____ to them.

Having Meals in an American Restaurant 🎧 079

When you go into an American restaurant, you get seated by a waiter/waitress. They give you the menu and show you to the table. The server brings you a glass of water and asks if you want anything else to drink and gets it for you. They give you a few minutes to decide what you want to eat, then come back and take the order to the cook. When the food is prepared they bring it back out and ask if there's anything else you need. They usually check back to see how you're doing a little while later. When you're done they bring you the check and you either give them money or a debit/credit card. They tender the bill and bring you back the change/card with a receipt. Standard tip is about 20-25% of the total depending on how good your service was.

Choose it! Match the pictures with the words in the box.

| tomato ketchup | tea spoon | salt | black pepper | knife |
| cup and saucer | steak sauce | paper napkins | fork | plate |

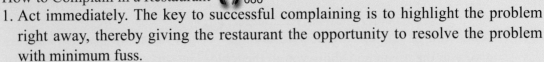

Check Points Lesson B

How to Complain in a Restaurant 🎧 080

1. Act immediately. The key to successful complaining is to highlight the problem right away, thereby giving the restaurant the opportunity to resolve the problem with minimum fuss.

2. Remain calm and objective. Discreetly call the waiter over, explain the problem, express your disappointment, and ask him or her to resolve the situation.

3. Suggest a resolution that matches your complaint. Would an apology be enough? Would you like your food replaced? Do you want a discount? Whatever it is, be sure to ask or politely suggest rather than demand.

4. If your concerns are not met with an acceptable resolution, ask politely to speak to the manager. Explain the problem to him or her, and state why you are not satisfied with how it has been resolved.

5. Reduce the tip. If other options proved fruitless, reducing the tip (or not leaving one at all) is a powerful way of expressing your displeasure.

Choose it! Match the pictures with the words in the box.

| shrimps | pizza | fish fillet | baked potato |
| oysters | spaghetti | steak | chicken legs |

_____

_____

_____

_____

_____

_____

_____

_____

100

Fast-food Restaurant & Bar

◆**Language Functions**

Placing Orders at a Fast-food Restaurant & At the Bar

◆**Sentence Patterns**

Expressions of Placing Orders at a Fast Food Restaurant & Expressions of Ordering Drinks at a Bar

◆**Vocabulary in Use**

Fast food & Drinks

Placing Orders at a Fast-food Restaurant

Part 1 Warm Up

Choose it! Check ☑ the correct answers.

1. Which is not a common meal in a fast food restaurant?

 ☐ Hamburger

 ☐ Pizza

 ☐ Steak

 ☐ Chicken sandwich

2. Beef burgers are made of pork. ☐ True ☐ False

3. Fries and chips are made of:

 ☐ Plastic

 ☐ Potato

 ☐ Chocolate

 ☐ Beef

4. Which is not a popular fast food restaurant drink?

 ☐ Milk shake

 ☐ Vodka

 ☐ Coca Cola

 ☐ Pepsi

5. What is a popular item with young children?

 ☐ Double beef burger

 ☐ Cheesecake

 ☐ Kid's meal

 ☐ Large fries

Part 2 Dialogue

Place orders at a fast-food restaurant. 082

Waiter: What can I get for you, ma'am?

Venus: Hello, may I have a double cheeseburger?

Waiter: With everything on it?

Venus: That sounds great.

Waiter: Do you want fries with your order?

Venus: May I get a large order of curly fries?

Waiter: Did you want something to drink?

Venus: Get me a medium Pepsi.

Waiter: And what can I get for you, sir?

David: Yes, I would like a fish burger, please.

Waiter: Would you like something to drink?

David: Yes, I would like a vanilla shake, please.

Waiter: Will that be all?

David: Yes, thank you.

Waiter: Your total is $16.20

David: Here's $20.00.

Waiter: Your change is $3.80. Thank you and come again!

Word Bank 081

curly fries (n.) 炸薯條
medium (adj.) 中等的
vanilla shake (n.) 香草奶昔

A For each sentence, check ☑ T (true) or F (false)

Venus is ordering a chicken burger.	T ☐	F ☐
Venus wants a medium fries with her order.	T ☐	F ☐
Venus also wants a medium Coke.	T ☐	F ☐
David is ordering a fish burger and a chocolate shake.	T ☐	F ☐
Venus' and David's meals cost them $16.20.	T ☐	F ☐

B Listen to the dialogue again, and then practice with your partner.

Part 3 Sentence Patterns *Expressions of Placing Order at a Fast Food Restaurant* 🎧 083

I'd like a cheeseburger, a big fries and a strawberry/ chocolate / vanilla shake.

Let me have a roast beef sandwich.

A hamburger and a large/ medium / small coke, please.

Would you like anything on the hamburger? / What sauce do you like?

Ketchup and mustard, please. / With mayonnaise, please.

Anything to drink? I'll have sprite without ice.

Large or small Coke/ 7 up / Pepsi / Sprite? Small coke, please.

Here or to go? For here/ To go, thanks.

A Look at the following fast-food menu and tell your partner what you like and dislike.

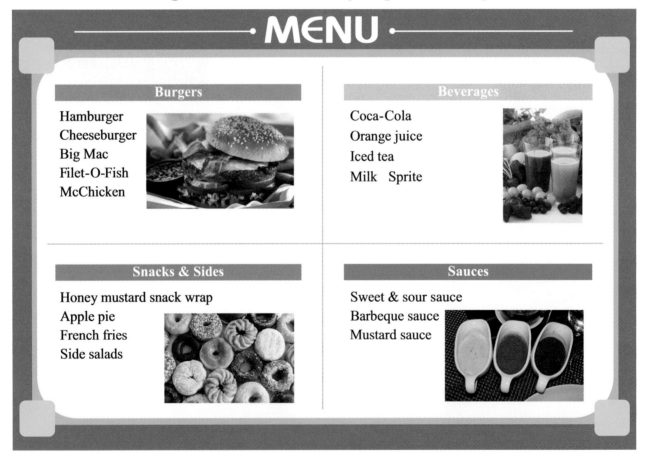

You like _____

You dislike _____

B Now work with your partners to use these sentence patterns to order food.

Part 4 Practice

Fill in the blanks! Use the words in the box to complete the following article.

bacon   cake   chicken   coffee   donut

fries   hamburger   hotdog   ice cream cone   juice

peach pie   pizza   salad   sandwich

soup   spaghetti   tea

Every Sunday I go to the local fast food restaurant with my friend, Daniel. We usually go for lunch. Sometimes we go for breakfast. For breakfast we usually have _____ and eggs. For lunch we usually have _____ and a _____ . Sometimes we have a _____ too. Sometimes we like to order a _____ or _____ and meatballs. Usually we have chocolate _____ for dessert. Sometimes we have a piece of _____ . Sam and I like the local fast food restaurant. The service and the food are good. Last week I went to a new fast food restaurant. I ordered a ham and cheese _____ . The waitress said they didn't have any ham so I ordered a _____ . I had _____ with my hamburger. My friend ordered a _____ . The waitress said they didn't have any hotdogs so he ordered a _____ dinner. He had a _____ with his chicken dinner. I wanted _____ for dessert but they didn't have any peach pie. I had a _____ for dessert. My friend had an _____ for dessert. After dinner I had a cup of _____ . My friend ordered an orange _____ but they didn't have any orange juice so he had a cup of _____ . I don't think we will go back to that restaurant. The service was not good.

Part 5 Role Play

Pair Work! Fill in the blanks and practice the completed dialogue with your partner.

Customer   Waiter

👤 Excuse me. I'd like _____, please.

👤 What kind of drink would you like?

👤 _____.

👤 Would you like a large _____ for 45 cents more?

👤 _____.

👤 For here or to go?

👤 _____.

👤 Alright. That's gonna be _____ dollars.

👤 Here you go.

👤 Thank you.

Part 1 Warm Up

Match it! Match each alcohol with its definition.

a. golden or clear alcohol, origin Mexico

b. various sweet alcohols

c. clear alcohol made from sugar cane, origin Caribbean

d. clear alcohol flavored with juniper berries

e. light brown alcohol made from grain, origin Scotland

f. clear alcohol made from grain or potato, origin Russia

Word Bank 084

gin (n.) 杜松子酒
liqueur (n.) 利口酒
　　　　（具甜味而芳香的烈酒）
rum (n.) 蘭姆酒‧甘蔗酒
　　　　（用甘蔗‧蜜糖等釀造）
vodka (n.) 伏特加酒
whisky (n.)（蘇格蘭產）威士忌酒
Tequila (n.) 龍舌蘭酒
　　　　（一種墨西哥產的蒸餾酒）

1 Gin

_____

2 Liqueur

_____

3 Rum

_____

4 Vodka

_____

5 Whisky

_____

6 Tequila

_____

Part 2 Dialogues

1. **Place orders at the bar.(1)** 🎧 086

Bartender: Hi there. What can I get for you?

    Guest: I need something cold.

Bartender: You've come to the right place.

    Guest: Do you have any specials?

Bartender: We have highballs for half price.

    Guest: Sorry, I meant for beer.

Bartender: Our beer special tonight is a pitcher of local draft with a half dozen wings for $12.99.

    Guest: I guess I should have brought a friend. I think I'll just have a Heineken for now.

Bartender: Sure, would you like that on tap or in a can?

    Guest: Do you have it in a bottle?

Bartender: No, I'm afraid we don't.

    Guest: That's okay. I'll take a pint.

Bartender: A pint of Heineken coming up.

    Guest: Actually, you better just make it a sleeve.

Bartender: Sure. And should I start you a tab?

    Guest: No, I'm driving. How much do I owe you?

Bartender: $5.25.

    Guest: Here's 6. Keep the change.

Bartender: Thank you.

Word Bank 🎧 085

highballs (n.) 高直杯子
pitcher (n.) 大水罐
draft beer (n.) 生啤酒
dozen (n.) 一打·12 個
(chicken) wings (n.) 雞翅
on tap(n.) 桶裝啤酒
pint (n.) 品脫
sleeve (n.)12 盎司的杯子
tab (n.) 帳單

A **Answer the following questions based on the dialogue above.**

(   ) 1. Which of the following is NOT on special tonight?

    (A) Jugs of beer   (B) Chicken wings   (C) Bottles of Heineken   (D) Mixed drinks

(   ) 2. What does the bartender give the guest to drink?

    (A) A glass of beer   (B) A bottle of beer   (C) A pitcher of beer(D) A can of beer

(   ) 3. How much money did the bartender make as a tip?

    (A) $6.00   (B) $5.25   (C) $0.75   (D) $0.25

B **Listen to the dialogue again, and then practice with your partner.**

2. Place orders at the bar.(2) 088

Edgar: I'd like a whiskey sour.

Bartender: Certainly sir, I'll get that straight away.
Here's your drink.
(Edgar takes a long sip)

Edgar: That's what I need. Do you have any snacks?

Bartender: Certainly, here are some peanuts and some savory crackers, and a napkin.

Edgar: Could I have a stir stick?

Bartender: Coming up... Here you are.

Edgar: Thanks. You know, I'm sorry to say this, but these snacks are awful.

Bartender: I'm terribly sorry about that, sir. What seems to be the matter?

Edgar: The peanuts are stale!

Bartender: I apologize, sir. I'll open a fresh can immediately.

Edgar: Thanks. Sorry to be in such a bad mood.

Bartender: That's quite alright. Can I get you another drink? This one's on the house.

Edgar: That's kind of you. Yes, I'll have another whiskey sour.

Bartender: Right away, sir.

Edgar: So how long have you worked at this bar?

Bartender: It's been about three years now. I love this job.

Word Bank 087

straight away (phr.) 立即;馬上
snack (n.) 點心
peanut (n.) 花生
savory (adj.) 好吃的
crackers (n.) 餅乾
awful (adj.) 糟糕的;可怕的
stale (adj.) 不新鮮的
immediately (adv.) 立即;馬上
on the house (phr.) 免費

A For each sentence, check ☑ T (true) or F (false)

The bar provides walnuts and savory crackers as snacks for customers.	T ☐	F ☐
The bartender offers Edgar a free drink.	T ☐	F ☐
The bartender has worked at the bar for three years.	T ☐	F ☐

B Listen to the dialogue again, and then practice with your partner.

Part 3 Sentence Patterns *Expressions of Ordering* 089

Questions you can ask the bartender/server:
What do you have on tap/on draft?
Do you have anything light on tap? (a light beer)
Do you have anything dark on draft?
Do you have any pale ales?
Do you have anything local?
Do you carry any import beers?

Ordering your drink:
We'd like a pitcher/jug of beer. (to share between 2 or more)
I'll have a bottle of _____ (beer name or beer type)
I'll have a glass of red wine. The house wine is fine. (the wine that the bar uses most often)
I'll have a glass of white.
We'd like a half liter of import white.
We'd like a liter of house red.

A Look at the following drinks list and tell your partner what you like.

Bar Drinks List

Vodka
Absolut Blue £2.60
Finlandia Classic £68.00 £2.60
Skyy £68.00 £2.60
Gin
Beefeaters £68.00 £2.60
Bombay Sapphire £2.80
Plymouth Gin £2.80
Rum
Bacardi Superior £68.00 £2.60
Bacardi 8yo £3.25
Woods Old Navy 100 Proof £3.30

Scotch De-Luxe Whisky
Ballantine's £80.00 £3.10
Johnnie Walker Black £3.20
Scotch Malt Whisky
Monkey Shoulder £3.50
Glenfiddich 15 yo £3.95
Balvenie Signature £4.10
Liqueurs
Malibu £2.50
Southern Comfort £2.85
Cointreau £2.95

I like _____ .

B Now work with your partners to order drinks.

_____

_____

_____

_____

Part 4 Practice

Choose it! Use the words in the box to complete the sentences.

get	glasses	pitcher	tap	call	sure
parts	potent	creation	part	serve	

1. Try this drink. It' my own _____.
2. Buying beer by the _____ is cheaper than buying it by the glass.
3. What kind of beer do you have on _____? (= on draught)
4. I'm not really _____ how to make that drink.
5. When the bartender says "Last _____!", it means that it's the last chance for customers to order drinks before the bar closes.
6. I'm warning you. This drink is really _____! (= strong)
7. It's two _____ orange juice and one _____ vodka.
8. I'm sorry but I can't _____ you since you're intoxicated (= drunk).
9. I've broken 5 _____ today.
10. What can I _____ you? = What would you like?

Part 5 Role Play

Pair work! Fill in the blanks and practice the completed dialogue with your partner.

Bartender: Good evening. What can I get for you?

    Guest: Do you have any _____?

Bartender: We have _____ for half price.

    Guest: I'll have _____.

Bartender: Our _____ special tonight is _____ for $_____.

    Guest: I think I'll just have _____ for now.

Bartender: A _____ coming up.

    Guest: How much do I owe you?

Bartender: $_____

    Guest: Here's _____. Keep the change.

Bartender: Thank you.

Fast food restaurant 🎧 090

A fast food restaurant, also known as a quick service restaurant (QSR) within the industry, is a specific type of restaurant characterized both by its fast food cuisine and by minimal table service. Food served in fast food restaurants typically caters to a "meat-sweet diet" and is offered from a limited menu; is cooked in bulk in advance and kept hot; is finished and packaged to order; and is usually available ready to take away, though seating may be provided.

Choose it! Write the correct word to describe what is being shown in each picture. Choose from the words in the box.

onion rings	soft drink	combo	sub	fries

I'd like some _____.

I'll have a _____.

I'll have a _____ meal.

_____.

I'll have a _____.

Order a drink at a bar 🎧091

Know what you want when the bartender asks you, especially if it's a busy night. The bartender doesn't have time to help you choose what you want. Look at the drinks behind the bar, read the board or look at the beer taps.

Ask for a specific type of liquor in your drink if you want a specific type of liquor. While your drink will be more expensive, it'll also taste better. If you don't specify a liquor, you'll get the house liquor, which is cheap.

Choose it! Choose the best response for each question.

Sentence Completion

( ) 1. Can we run a tab?
    (A) Sure, I'll start one for you.   (B) That'll be $5, please.
    (C) No, we don't have one.

( ) 2. What kind of beer do you have on tap?
    (A) Guinness and Kilkenny.   (B) Bottled beer or draught beer?
    (C)We're all out of bottled beer.

( ) 3. You got any appetizers/snacks?
    (A) Our special today is Chicken Florentine.
    (B) We've got chips, fries, and peanuts.
    (C) We have Guinness and Budweiser on tap.

( ) 4. Can I smoke at the bar?
    (A) No, you're not allowed to smoke anywhere inside the club.
    (B) Thanks, but I don't smoke.
    (C) Sure, thanks.

( ) 5. Can I get another round?
    (A) What would you like?
    (B) Yes, we'll move you to another table right away.
    (C) Sure. That was two Coronas and a glass of red wine, right?

Sightseeing

◆**Language Functions**

Tourist Information & Tours

◆**Sentence Patterns**

Expressions of Asking for Tourist Information &
Expressions of Tour Guides and Tourists

◆**Vocabulary in Use**

Sightseeing Attractions and Activities

Part 1 Warm Up

A Match the pictures with the words in the box.

temple	museum	castle	cinema
aquarium	amusement park	concert	casino

Part 2 **Dialogues**

1. At the tourist information center 093

Jack: Hi, do you have any free maps of the city?

Worker: Yes, we do. And we also have a free information booklet.

Jack: Great. Could we have one, please?

Worker: Sure, here you go.

Jack: We're only here for one day. What do you recommend that we see?

Worker: Well, you can walk down Sunset Boulevard. It has some beautiful historic architecture, and some good museums. Actually, that whole neighborhood is very interesting.

Jack: What's that neighborhood called?

Worker: Uptown. When you go out, just turn right and in about three blocks you'll come to Sunset Boulevard.

Jack: Great! We'll check it out.

Word Bank 092

booklet (n.) 小冊子
Boulevard(n.) 林蔭大道
historic (adj.) 歷史上著名的
architecture (n.) 建築物
neighborhood (n.) 鄰近地區

A **For each sentence, check ☑ T (true) or F (false)**

Both maps of city and information booklets are free at the tourist information center.	T ☐	F ☐
The worker at the tourist information center recommends that Jack should visit the uptown area around Sunset Boulevard.	T ☐	F ☐
Sunset Boulevard is far from where Jack is now.	T ☐	F ☐

B **Listen to the dialogue again, and then practice with your partner.**

2. Ask about some information at a museum  095

Dennis: Hello. What time does the museum close today?

Museum worker: The museum closes at 7:00 p.m.

Dennis: And what time does it open tomorrow?

Museum worker: The museum opens at 9:00 a.m.

Dennis: And how much is the admission?

Museum worker: The admission fee is $8. $5 if you're a student.

Dennis: And are there any special exhibitions on right now?

Museum worker: Yes, there's a special exhibition of Edward Hopper's early paintings.

Dennis: Is this included in the price of admission?

Museum worker: No, there's a separate $5 charge for the exhibition.

Word Bank 094

admission (n.) 入場券,門票
exhibition (n.) 展覽;展覽會
painting (n.) 繪畫
separate (adj.) 個別的,不同的

A For each sentence, check ☑ T (true) or F (false)

The museum opens at 7:00 a.m.	T ☐	F ☐
The admission fee for students is $5.	T ☐	F ☐
Visitors need to pay $5 for the exhibition of Edward Hopper's early paintings.	T ☐	F ☐

B Listen to the dialogue again, and then practice with your partner.

Part 3 Sentence Patterns *Expressions of Asking and Giving Tourist Information* 🎧096

Questions asked by tourists:
Where can I get some tourist information?
Can I have a map of this city/ brochure of the sightseeing tours?
Which tour would you recommend?
Do you have a day tour for Cambridge?

Answers by staff at the Tourist Information Center:
Here is a guidebook and some pamphlets supplying information about the city.
We have information brochures on hotels, restaurants, department stores, and places of entertainment.
I highly recommend tour No. 2 the city tour.
This is a cultural tour, and includes the municipal museum and the art gallery.

A Work with your partner to discuss what the tours and activities in the following box are and which you like.

Aquarium	Art museum	Canyon	Casino	Castle	Concert
Helicopter tour	Horseback riding	Hot spring	Ocean Park	Snorkeling	Skydiving
Surfing	Theme Park	Water skiing	Zoo	Pyramid	

B Now work with your partners to ask and give tourist information.

_____

_____

_____

_____

Part 4 Practice

Information for visitors! Fill in the following information according to what you find on the Internet in regard to the site you choose.

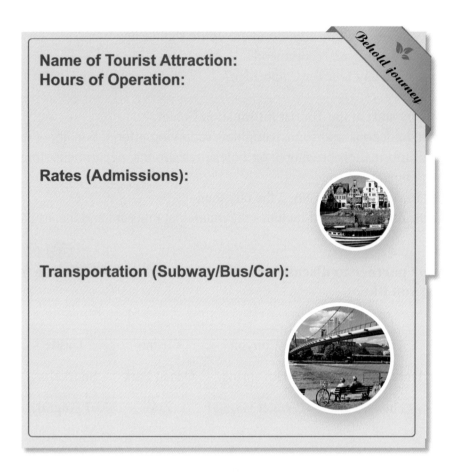

Name of Tourist Attraction:
Hours of Operation:

Rates (Admissions):

Transportation (Subway/Bus/Car):

Behold journey

Part 5 Role Play

Pair work! Fill in the blanks and practice the completed dialogue with your partner.

👤 Tourist   👤 Security Officer

👤 Where can I buy an _____ ticket?

👤 The ticket _____ is through the gate over there on your _____.

👤 Thank you. By the way, is there any special _____ in this _____?

👤 Well, let's see, there's the _____.

👤 Sounds _____. Is the _____ included in the cost of admission?

👤 No, it's not. There's an additional _____ dollar(s) for the _____.

👤 I see. Thank you for the information.

👤 You're welcome. And have _____!

Part 1 Warm Up

Match the pictures with the words in the box.

snorkeling	surfing	water skiing	scuba diving
skiing	skydiving	bungee jump	horseback riding

Part 2 Dialogues

1. **Tour guide announcement** 098

Guide: If you have any questions while we're going along, please don't hesitate to ask.

Man: I have a question actually.

Guide: Sure, what's that?

Man: Where's the best place to have dinner around here?

Guide: There are so many good restaurants. My personal favorite is Meow Meow Kitchen.

Man: How do we get there?

Guide: I'll point it out when we pass it. It's going to come up on your right in a few minutes.

Woman: My son wants to know if we're going to be passing any night markets today.

Guide: Night markets. No, I'm afraid the night markets are further into the downtown. We're going to be staying near the harbor today. I can give you a map of the city, though. It shows where all of the night markets are.

Word Bank  097

hesitate (n.) 躊躇；猶豫
point out (phr.) 指出
harbor (n.) 港灣 · 海港

A For each sentence, check ☑ T (true) or F (false)

A man is asking the guide to recommend a best restaurant for lunch.	T ☐	F ☐
The Meow Meow Kitchen is quite far away where they are now.	T ☐	F ☐
They are going to stay at a hotel near a night market.	T ☐	F ☐

B Listen to the dialogue again, and then practice with your partner.

2. Tour guide  🎧 100

Hello everyone. My name is Sophia. On behalf of Happy Tours I'd like to welcome you all to Keelung. The bus ride to your hotel will take about twenty minutes. Right now I'd like to take a minute to familiarize you with the area and discuss some brief safety precautions. Firstly, I ask that you remain seated until we reach our destination. Secondly, please realize that it is against the law to get drunk in public. Enjoy your vacation, but do not drink and drive.

I promise you are going to enjoy your stay here in Keelung. This is a beautiful, prosperous city where you can relax, sit by the beach, enjoy great seafood and feel very safe. You can walk into the downtown and enjoy the local cuisines at the night market or take a moonlit walk along the harbor. Please do not swim here. This is not a safe place to swim because there are strong surges.

A For each sentence, check ☑ T (true) or F (false)

Word Bank 🎧 099

on behalf of (phr.) 代表
familiarize... with (phr.) 使熟悉；使親近
area (n.) 地區，區域
precaution (n.) 預防；警惕
realize (v.) 領悟，了解
against (prep.) 反對；違反
in public (phr.) 公開地；公然
promise (v.) 允諾，答應
prosperous (adj.) 興旺的；繁榮的
relax (v.) 使輕鬆
downtown (n.) 城市商業區，鬧區
cuisine (n.) 菜餚
moonlit (adj.) 月光照耀的
along (prep.) 沿著；順著
surge (n.) 大浪，波濤

Sophia is a tour guide of Happy Tours. T ☐ F ☐

Tourists can enjoy the local cuisines at restaurants in Keelung. T ☐ F ☐

The harbor is a safe place to swim because there are strong surges. T ☐ F ☐

B Listen to the dialogue again, and then practice with your partner.

Part 3 Sentence Patterns *Expressions of Tour Guides and Tourists* 🎧 101

Tour Guides:
In front of you is the Meow Meow Kitchen.
On your right/left you will see the Sun Yat-sen Memorial Hall.
If you look up you will notice the Taipei 101 is not far away from us.
We are now coming up to the hotel we'll stay for overnight.

Tourist Questions:
Is that the Confucius Temple you were talking about?
Are we going to pass the night market?
I don't see it. Can you point it out again?
Will we see it on the way back?

A **Use the tourist attractions in the box in each of the following sentences and then practice with your partner.**

Gallery

Museum

Castle

Theme Park

Zoo

Temple

Tower

Palace

1. In front of you is _____.
2. On your right you will see _____.
3. If you look up you will notice _____ is not far away from us.
4. We are now coming up _____.
5. Is that _____ you were talking about?
6. Are we going to pass _____?

Souvenir shop

Shopping Mall

Tourism English

B Now make a short dialogue between a tour guide and a tourist with your partner.

_____

_____

_____

_____

Part 4 Practice

Choose it! Fill in the following blanks with correct words in the box.

recommend	as well as	lobby	activities
offers	charge	advice	percent

Happy Tours _____ a variety of special discounts depending on your travel plans. We have city tours, _____ guided whale boat tours, and fishing charters. There will be a short information session at 9 a.m. in the _____ of the hotel tomorrow where you can learn all about these offers. We _____ that you do not purchase packages from street vendors as they are not always 100 _____ reliable. They also may _____ you more than what they say. Please take my _____ and allow Happy Tours to book all of your day trips and _____ while you are here.

Part 5 Role Play

Pair work! Fill in the blanks and practice the completed dialogue with your partner.

Clement: I'd like to book _____ for "Les Miserables". Are there any seats available?

　Clerk: We're sorry, it's all sold out for tonight.

Clement: Then, can I reserve the seats for this coming _____ night?

　Clerk: Oh, sure. We still have a few seats in the _____.

Clement: That sounds fine. How much are the tickets?

　Clerk: It's _____ per person. How many tickets would you like to reserve?

Clement: _____, please. When does the show start?

　Clerk: It starts at _____.

Tourist information center 🎧 102

A visitor center, visitor information center, tourist information center, is a physical location that provides tourist information to the visitors who tour the place or area locally. It may be a visitor center at a specific attraction or place of interest, such as a landmark, national park, national forest, or state park, providing information (such as trail maps, and about camp sites, staff contact, restrooms, etc.) and in-depth educational exhibits and artifact displays (for cxample, about natural or cultural history).

Choose it! Choose the correct, best responses according to the context of the conversation.

Sentence Completion

(　) 1. Tourist: Hello. What time _____ the museum close today?
(A) when　　　　(B) then　　　　(C) does

(　) 2. Museum worker: The museum closes at 7:00 PM.
　　　　　Tourist: And what time _____ tomorrow?
(A) does it open　　(B) it opens　　(C) opening

(　) 3. Museum worker: The museum opens at 9:00 AM.
　　　　　Tourist: And _____ is the admission?
(A) what money　　(B) what cost　　(C) how much

(　) 4. Museum worker: The admission fee is $8... $5 if you're a student.
　　　　　Tourist: And are there any special exhibitions _____ right now?
(A) off　　　　(B) on　　　　(C) at

(　) 5. Museum worker: Yes, there's a special exhibition of Edward Hopper's early paintings.
　　　　　Tourist: Is this _____ in the price of admission?
(A) a cost　　　(B) included　　(C) with
Museum worker: No, there's a separate $5 charge for the exhibition.

129

Tour guide 🎧103

The role of tour guide is basically to provide the best tourist packages to the people who are interested to spend their holidays and want to go to some different places. It is the responsibility of tour guide to make the best possible travel arrangements for their customers and make their whole trip enjoyable.

Choose it! Choose the correct, best responses according to the context of the conversation.

Sentence Completion

( ) 1. Tourist A: Does the _____ leave from here?
    (A) sightseeing voyage   (B) sightseeing journey
    (C) sightseeing tour

( ) 2. Tourist B: Yes, I think so. We're just waiting for the tour guide to arrive.
    Tourist A: Isn't the tour _____ to start at 4:30?
    (A) made   (B) supposed   (C) have

( ) 3. Tourist B: Yes, it is. I guess the tour guide is running a little late.
               (5 minutes later)
    Tour guide: I'm sorry everyone, the 4:30 p.m. tour has been cancelled. We're having some mechanical problems with our bus.
     Tourist A: So there won't be _____ tours today?
    (A) another   (B) the   (C) any more

( ) 4. Tour guide: I'm not sure right now. We'll have to wait and see...
    Tourist A: How long _____?
    (A) do we have to wait   (B) to wait   (C) is the waiting

( ) 5. Tour guide: I'm not sure. They're fixing the bus right now. If they don't fix it in 30 minutes, I'll give all of you your money back.
    Tourist A: And how long does _____ once it starts?
    (A) the last tour   (B) the tour last   (C) the time
    Tour guide: About one hour.

Shopping

◆**Language Functions**

Buying Clothing and Souvenirs & Refunding and Bargaining

◆**Sentence Patterns**

Expressions of Buying Clothing & Expressions of Bargaining

◆**Vocabulary in Use**

Clothing & Shops

Buying Clothing and Souvenirs

Part 1 Warm Up

Choose it! Choose the words in the box to answer the following questions.

tie

cap

a suit

a scarf

a dress

a jacket

1. What does a man wear if he goes to a meeting?_____
2. What does a lady wear if she goes to a wedding party?_____
3. If a man goes to a wedding, he wears a white suit with a black _____.
4. What do you put on your head?_____
5. What do you wear round your neck in winter?_____
6. What do you wear when it is cold?_____

Part 2 Dialogues

1. **Buy clothing** 105

Clerk: May I help you, sir?

Steven: Yes, please. I'm looking for a cotton polo shirt.

Clerk: How about this one?

Steven: I like the design, but don't particularly care for the color. Do you have that in other colors, too?

Clerk: Well, they come in blue, yellow, purple, red and green. Will a blue one do?

Steven: Yes. I prefer blue. And may I see a yellow one, too?

Clerk: Here you are, sir. Would you like to try it on? The fitting rooms are over there.

Steven: Thanks.

Clerk: That blue polo shirt looks really nice on you!

Steven: Well, I'll take it.

Clerk: Thank you. Do you need anything to go with the shirt?

Steven: No, that will be all.

Clerk: OK. That's $ 42, please.

Steven: Oh, I'll pay by credit card then. Here you go.

Clerk: Thank you.

Word Bank 104

cotton (n.) 棉．棉花
particular (adj.) 特定的；特別的
care for (phr.) 喜歡
fitting room (n.) 服裝店的試衣室
go with (phr.) 搭配

A For each sentence, check ☑ T (true) or F (false)

Steven is particularly looking for a yellow polo shirt.	T ☐	F ☐
The clerk suggests that Steven take the blue polo shirt.	T ☐	F ☐
Steven pays by traveler's checks.	T ☐	F ☐

B Listen to the dialogue again, and then practice with your partner.

Tourism English

2. **Buying souvenirs** 107

Clerk: Do you need any help, sir?

Jack: Well, I'm looking for a gift for my mother.

Clerk: May I suggest something? This dinnerware set is perfect for mothers.

Jack: Very nice! How much is it?

Clerk: It is $525.

Jack: It's a little over my budget. Do you have something less expensive?

Clerk: Well, how about this set, sir? It's on sale right now. $300, down from $450. It's a bargain.

Jack: Hmm... OK. I'll take it. Can you gift-wrap that?

Clerk: Certainly, sir. How would you like to pay?

Jack: I'll pay for it with my VISA.

Clerk: It's all yours after you sign here, please.

Jack: You've been so helpful. Thank you.

Clerk: Have a nice day, and thank you for shopping here.

Word Bank 106

dinnerware (n.) 整套的餐具
budget (n.) 預算
bargain (n.) 廉價；便宜貨
gift-wrap (v.) 用包裝紙包裝

A For each sentence, check ☑ T (true) or F (false)

Jack is buying a dinnerware set for his mother.	T ☐	F ☐
The dinnerware set costs Jack $450.	T ☐	F ☐
Jack is paying by cash for the gift.	T ☐	F ☐

B Listen to the dialogue again, and then practice with your partner.

Part 3 **Sentence Patterns** *Expressions of Buying Clothing* 108

Buying clothing:
Where's the section for men's / ladies' wear?
I'm looking for a shirt/ skirt / blue jeans.
What size do you take / wear? I usually wear a size 6.
My waistline is twenty-four inches.
Do you have something smaller / bigger of this style?
Do you have the same design in _____ (color)?
It's a little loose / tight around the waist.
This shirt is a little too long / short / large / small for me.

Buying souvenirs:
I'm looking for a gift for my mother.
Could you recommend a gift for a young woman?

A **Discuss with your partner what the items in the box are and which you like to buy**

Blouse	Bra	Pajamas	Polo shirt	Sportswear	Sweater	Swimsuit	Underwear
Pants	Panties	Flats	High-heeled shoes	Riding boots	Sandals	Sports shoes	Shorts

B **Now work with your partners to use these sentence patterns to buy clothing & souvenirs**

_____

_____

_____

_____

Part 4 Practice

A How to talk about prices!

For example: $10.75
We don't need to say: ten dollars and seventy five cents. We just say: ten seventy five.
1. Now try to read the following prices.

$3.80 $9.75 $8.05 $1.50 $2.89 $26.30 $33.93

$23.00 $47.35 $103.65 $145.25

2. Dictate the amounts in random order and have your partner write them.

B Fill in the blanks of the following five short dialogues and practice them with your partner

Store clerk: Thank you. Do you need anything to go with the shirt?
  Customer: No, that will be all.
Store clerk: OK. That's $ _____, please.

Store clerk: Well, how about this set, sir? It's on sale right now. $ _____, down from $ _____.
                 It's a bargain.

Store clerk: May I suggest something? This dinnerware set is perfect for mother.
  Customer: Very nice! How much is it?
Store clerk: It is $ _____.

  Customer: How much are these postcards?
Store clerk: They're 10 for $ _____.

Store clerk: Sixty-five! Come on, lady. You've got to be kidding. I paid more than that for it
                 myself. Take it for $ _____. It's worth every penny.
  Customer: Well, maybe I could give you $ _____.

Part 5 Role Play

Pair work! Fill in the blanks and practice the completed dialogue with your partners.

Clerk   Kobe

👩 Can I help you?

🧑 Yes, how much is that _____?

👩 It's $_____.

🧑 Can I try it _____?

👩 Yes, what size are you?

🧑 I don't know.

👩 Ok, try a size _____. The _____ room is over there.

(Kobe puts on the _____. It's too small)

🧑 Do you have it in a _____ size?

👩 Yes, here you are.

🧑 Thank you.

👩 How was it?

🧑 I'll take it.

Refunding and Bargaining

Part 1 Warm Up

A What may you say while bargaining with a store clerk?

☐ How much does it cost?
☐ Can you lower the price?
☐ Can you give me a discount ?
☐ That's too expensive, how about 15 dollars?
☐ How much will that be altogether ?

B Check ☑ the following scenarios that you can get refunds.

☐ You bought a new flat screen TV, but when you switch it on, the screen is blank.

☐ You bought some fish fillets from a supermarket, but they smell bad.

☐ You bought some apples from a fruit shop but when you cut them open they are rotten inside.

☐ You bought a PC game but it won't load on your computer even though the box says it should.

☐ You bought a new microwave with a one-year warranty two years ago. You unpacked it only recently, to find it doesn't work.

Part 2 Dialogues

1. Returning shirts 110

Shop clerk: Can I help you?

Customer: Yes. I'd like to return these shirts.

Shop clerk: May I ask why you're returning them?

Customer: I bought them for my husband, but they're too short.

Shop clerk: Do you have the receipt?

Customer: Yes, here it is.

Shop clerk: I'm sorry. These shirts were on sale. There are no refunds on sale items. You can exchange them for something else or we can give you a credit note.

Customer: Do you have shirts in a larger size?

Shop clerk: I'm afraid they have sold out.

Customer: Okay, I'll take a credit note. How long is it good for?

Shop clerk: It's good for a year.

Customer: Okay. I'll come back next week and see if I can find something else he might like.

Word Bank 109

receipt (n.) 收據
refund (v.) 退還 ; (n.) 退款
credit note (n.) 賒欠憑證

A For each sentence, check ☑ T (true) or F (false)

The customer wants to get a refund for the shirts she bought.	T ☐	F ☐
The clerk asks the customer to exchange shirts for something else.	T ☐	F ☐
The customer won't come back to the store again.	T ☐	F ☐

B Listen to the dialogue again, and then practice with your partner

Tourism English

2. Bargaining 🎧 112

Adeline: Excuse me. How much do you want for this vase?

Clerk: Let's see. Hmm... That's an outstanding piece of glass in perfect shape. It's worth 150 bucks. I'm only asking $115.

Adeline: A hundred and fifteen dollars?

Clerk: Yeah, it's a real bargain.

Adeline: Oh I'm sure it is. But I can't afford that.

Clerk: Well, look. I'll make it an even $100. I can't go any lower than that.

Adeline: I'll give you $65.

Clerk: Sixty-five! Come on, lady. You've got to be kidding. I paid more than that for it myself. Take it for $90. It's worth every penny.

Adeline: Well, maybe I could give you $75.

Clerk: Eighty-five. That's my final price.

Adeline: OK. Eighty-five.

Clerk: Let me wrap it up for you. There you are, lady... a real bargain.

Adeline: Yeah, thanks a lot.

Word Bank 🎧 111

outstanding (adj.) 傑出的
worth (v.) 有 (...的) 價值．值
buck (n.) (美俚語) 元
afford (v.) 買得起
It's a shame. 遺憾！多可惜啊！
penny (n.) (美國) 一分；一分硬幣
kidding (adj.) 開玩笑
final (adj.) 最後的；最終的

A For each sentence, check ✓ T (true) or F (false)

Adeline is bargaining with the clerk on a vase.	T ☐	F ☐
The clerk says she paid more than $100 for the vase herself.	T ☐	F ☐
The final price for the vase is $75.	T ☐	F ☐

B Listen to the dialogue again, and then practice with your partne

Part 3 Sentence Patterns *Expressions of Refunding and Bargaining* 🎧 113

Guest:
It is too expensive for me. I can't afford it.
I'll be buying more, couldn't you knock off a little bit more?
You're overcharging me.
Can you give me a discount?
I'd like to return these shirts.
Could I have a refund?

Store clerk:
I'm afraid the prices are fixed in this store.
I can give a 10% discount.
Five hundred, and that's final.
I'm sorry, we're unable to give any price reduction.
There are no refunds on sale items.
Do you have the receipt?

A Match the words or expressions below with the correct meaning on the right.

1. return	available to buy
2. on sale	give back
3. refund	swap
4. exchange	proof of purchase
5. receipt	reduced price
6. valid	give back money
7. for sale	able to use
8. credit note	note allowing customer to purchase goods to the value specified

B Now work with your partners to make short dialogues about bargaining and refunding.

Part 4 Practice

Choose it! Fill in the following blanks with correct words in the box.

afford	expensive	give you a discount	available	for sale
How much	save	second-hand	priceless	ripped off

1. I'd like to buy this sweater, but it is too _____!

2. Is this item _____? No sorry, we're out of stock.

3. This box is not _____, you cannot buy it.

4. _____ is it, please? That's very cheap, only 5 dollars!

5. She will have to _____ money if she wants to buy a new car.

6. I always buy _____ books.

7. This diamond is _____!

8. Don't spend money on clothes, you can't _____ it.

9. Ask the shop assistant if she can _____.

10. You said you paid 25 € for this? I can't believe it! You were _____!

Part 5 Role Play

Pair work! **Fill in the blanks and practice the completed dialogue with your partner.**

🌑 Clerk   🌑 David

🌑 Good _____, can I help you?

🌑 I hope so. I'm looking for a _____.

🌑 The _____ is on special offer this week.

🌑 How much is it?

🌑 Only $_____.

🌑 It's a little expensive. Do you have a _____ one?

🌑 Yes. This one's only $_____

🌑 What make is it?

🌑 It's a _____.

🌑 I like it, but it's still a little too expensive. Is there any chance of a _____?

🌑 Hmm...., OK, we can do it for $_____.

🌑 Great, I'll take it. Do you accept _____?

🌑 Yes we do.

Buy Clothes That Fit 🎧 114
Understand clothing designs. Every garment will fit differently, because of the designer, pattern, and manufacturer. The sooner that you accept this, the better; what might be a size 8 in one brand may well be a size 6 or 10 in another.
Look what styles look best for your physique. This will be learned through trial and error; so do try on those clothes and don't just grab and buy!

Choose it! Match the pictures with the words in the box.

neckties	jeans	jacket	skirt
shirt	dress	scarf	sweater

_____

_____

_____

_____

_____

_____

_____

_____

Bargaining 🎧 115
Initiating the negotiation can be tricky. If an item is marked with a price, you're ahead of the game. To find out the desired price, try to avoid asking dead-end questions like, "How much is this?" Instead, opt for a more open phrasing such as, "What are you asking for this?" Most importantly, be confident. When you come across as assertive, the seller will take notice.

Choose it! Match the pictures with the words in the box.

| florist store | jewelry store | bakery | hardware store |
| cosmetics store | pet store | electrics store | pharmacy |

Bank

◆Language Functions

Cashing Traveler's Checks and Changing
Currency & Open a Bank Account

◆Sentence Patterns

Expressions of Cashing Traveler's Checks and
Changing Currency & Expressions of Making a
Deposit and Withdrawing Money at a Bank

◆Vocabulary in Use

Currencies & Bank

Part 1 Warm Up

Choose it! Use the words in the box to complete the sentences. Change the forms when necessary.

cash	checkbook	traveler's checks	card	deposited

1. Jane's salary is _____ directly into her bank account.

2. Banks give customers a _____ which allows them to write checks to pay for goods and services

3. A bank _____ allows customers to withdraw cash from an ATM.

4. Leila wants to _____ her check because she needs the money right away.

5. I am going to buy _____ because I don't want to carry cash when I go to Paris.

Part 2 Dialogue 117

Janet: Good morning. Could I change 300 dollars worth of U.S. traveler's checks into Canadian dollars?

Teller: Canadian dollars?

Janet: Yes, that's correct. By the way, what's today's rate?

Teller: Today's rate 1 US dollar is equivalent to 1.20 Canadian. May I see your passport, please?

Janet: Yeah, of course. Here it is.

Teller: Thanks so much. And would you please sign and date all the checks as well?

Janet: All right.

(Janet signs and dates all the checks)

Teller: Thank you, ma'am. Here's your $360.00 dollars.

A For each sentence, check ☑ **T (true) or F (false)**

> **Word Bank** 116
>
> Canadian (adj.) 加拿大的
> by the way (phr.) 順便提起
> rate (n.) 比率
> equivalent (adj.) 相等的
> sign (v.) 簽名
> date (v.) 註明日期於

	T	F
Janet is trying to cash her traveler's checks.	T ☐	F ☐
The Canadian dollar is worth more than the US dollar.	T ☐	F ☐
Janet is required to show her passport and sign her name on the traveler's checks.	T ☐	F ☐

B Listen to the dialogue again, and then practice with your partner.

Part 3 Sentence Patterns *Expressions of Cashing Traveler's Checks and Changing Currency* 🎧118

I'd like to change...into...
I'd like to change this a hundred dollar traveler's check into N.T. dollars.
I'd like to change 5,000 N.T. dollars into U.S. dollars / British pounds / Japanese yen?

How many ···dollars/pounds/yens to···dollars/pounds/yens?
How many N.T. dollars to a U.S. dollar? Thirty and twenty six cents to a U.S dollar.
How would you like···?
How would you like the bills? All of it in tens, please.

Can you break....?
Can you break this bill into small change?
Can you give me...in...?
Can you give me twenty dollars in ones?

Now work with your partners to use these sentence patterns to practice cashing traveler's checks and changing currency at a bank.

Part 4 Practice

Credit Card Cancellation Letter!

Unscramble the sentences of the following credit card cancellation letter to a bank with numbers 1, 2, 3....

____ and will not be using the credit card so do not wish to incur the annual fee.

____ The card is a Platinum Card with the number: 4567999901110222, valid until 12/20.

____ Dear Sir/Madam

____ If there is any other information you need, please do not hesitate to contact us at the above e-mail address.

____ I am writing this letter to request the cancellation of mine and my wife's Chinatrust credit card.

____ The reason is that we are living in the US for the foreseeable future,

Yours Faithfully

Clement Chen

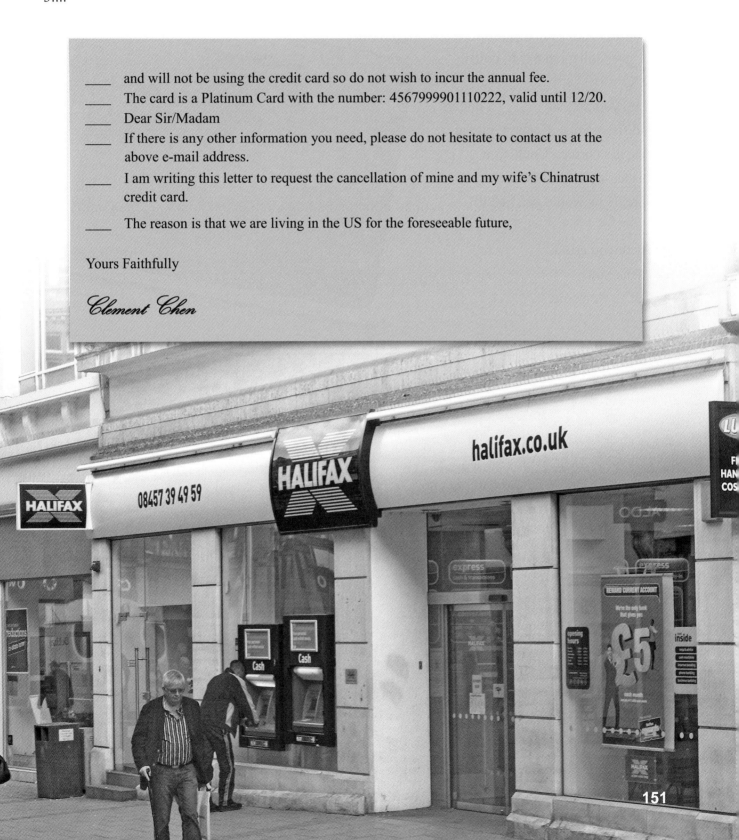

Tourism English

Part 5 Role Play

Pair work! Fill in the blanks and practice the completed dialogue with your partner.

 Bank teller   Tourist

I'd like to change _____ dollars into U.S. dollars, please. What's today's rate?

_____ dollars to a U.S. dollar.

O.K.

Here you are, sir. _____ dollars and fifty cents. Count it, please.

Yes, it's correct. Could you _____ this ten-dollar bill for me?

Sure. How would you like it?

_____.

There you go.

Thank you.

You're welcome.

Open a Bank Account

Part 1 Warm Up

A Check ☑ the documentes that are needed to open a personal bank account in your country?

☐ driver's license   ☐ state-issued ID   ☐ Social Security number

☐ proof of your address   ☐ current email address

B Discuss the following questions in a group and then share your ideas with your classmates.

1. Do you think banks help people to save money?
2. Is it easy or difficult to open an account with a bank in your country?
3. How did you choose your bank?

Part 2 Dialogues

1. **Open a Bank Account** 🎧 120

Bank Teller: How are you doing today?

Cindy: Great. Thanks.

Bank Teller: What can I help you with?

Cindy: I'd like to open a bank account, please.

Bank Teller: Certainly. Do you have some form of identification?

Cindy: Yes, I have a passport. Is that OK?

Bank Teller: Yes. We also need proof of your current address. Do you have a utility bill or your driver's license with you?

Cindy: I've got my driver's license.

Bank Teller: That's fine. What kind of account would you like to open?

Cindy: I need a checking account.

Bank Teller: Would you also like to open a savings account?

Cindy: That would be great.

Bank Teller: To open these accounts, you will need to make a deposit of at least $50.

Cindy: I want to deposit $400.

Bank Teller: I'll set up your accounts for you right now.

Cindy: Make sure to put $200 in each account.

> **Word Bank** 🎧 119
>
> account (n.) 帳戶
> proof (n.) 證明
> current (adj.) 現時的,當前的
> address (n.) 住址·地址
> checking account 支票戶頭
> savings account 儲蓄存款戶頭
> deposit (n.) 存款;(v.) 存放(銀行等)
> utility (n.) 公用事業
> bill (n.) 帳單
> set up (phr.) 建立
> make sure (phr.) 確定
> each (adj.) 每一個

A For each sentence, check ☑ T (true) or F (false)

The bank teller asks for Cindy's identification card.	T ☐	F ☐
Cindy uses her passport as her ID.	T ☐	F ☐
Cindy wants to open more than one account.	T ☐	F ☐
Cindy asks for a checking account and a credit card.	T ☐	F ☐

B Listen to the dialogue again, and then practice with your partner.

2. Problems with the ATM 122

James: Sorry, could you help me please? I had some problems with the ATM. My credit card has been swallowed.

Bank teller: Did it arrive before you entered your secret PIN code or after?

James: Before.

Bank teller: Before? Are you sure?

James: Yes, I am! And the screen changed telling me 'Sorry, this ATM is currently unavailable' but I don't know the meaning.

Bank teller: Ah I see. It was the daily safeguarding time. I think my colleague collected your card. Here it is but could you show me your identity card? ..... That's OK and your bank allowed the transaction.

James: Great!

Bank teller: In five minutes you'll be able to use the machine.

James: Thank you very much, bye.

A Answer the following questions according to the dialogue above.

Word Bank 121

ATM = Automated Teller Machine,
Automatic Teller Machine 自動存提款機；自動出納機
swallow (v.) 吞下；嚥下
screen (n.) 銀幕；(電視的) 螢光幕
PIN= personal identification number 個人識別號
unavailable (adj.) 無法利用的
safeguarding (adj.) 保護的；防衛的
colleague (n.) 同事
collect (v.) 收集
identity (n.) 身分
allow (v.) 允許，准許
transaction (n.) 交易；辦理

1. What were James' problems?
2. What's wrong with the ATM?

B Listen to the dialogue again, and then practice with your partner.

Part 3 Sentence Patterns *Expressions of Making a Deposit and Withdrawing Money at a Bank* 🎧 123

Customer
I'd like to make a deposit into my checking /savings account, please.
I'd like to withdraw some money from my savings account.

Bank teller
Can I have your bankcard please? Sure. Here it is.
Do you have a deposit slip filled out? Yes, here it is, with my paycheck.
Please complete this withdrawal slip, with your name, account number and amount of withdrawal.

A Fill in the following blanks.

1
A: Hello Miss. I want to save money to my bank account?
B: OK, can you tell me your account number?
A: Yes, it 533800001238888, I want to make _____ at your bank.

2
A: Can I help you?
B: Yes, I'd like to deposit this check.
A: Please fill out a _____ and be sure to endorse the check on the back.

3
A: Could I help you?
B: Yes. I want to withdraw some money from my bank account.
A: OK, Please fill out a _____. The red one.
B: Thanks, I will finish right now.

B Now work with your partners to use these sentence patterns to practice making a deposit and withdrawing money at a bank.

_____

_____

_____

_____

Part 4 Practice

A Use the words in the box to fill in the following blanks of an ATM.

display screen	speaker	cash dispenser	screen buttons
receipt printer	keypad	card reader	deposit slot

Part 5 Role Play

Pair work! Fill in the blanks and practice the completed dialogue with your partner.

Bank teller: Could I help you?

Clement: Yes, please. I want to _____ in your bank. What kind of accounts can I open here?

Bank teller: Our bank offer _____ and _____ for individuals.

Clement: I want a _____ account.

Bank teller: Please give me your ID card or _____?

Clement: OK. Here _____.

Bank teller: Let me see. Now I'll open a new account for you, please wait a second.

Clement: Thanks.

Bank teller: Sir, your card is OK, here _____.

Clement: _____ thanks.

Traveler's checks 124

Travelers like traveler's checks because of the safety features. When you purchase traveler's checks, you are required to sign each check twice -- once while the supplier watches and then again in view of the merchandiser when using the checks to make a purchase. If you lose traveler's checks, you need only contact the issuer of the checks, present them with the serial number of your checks, and they can often help you replace your checks within 24 hours with no funds lost to you.

Recognize it! Match the names of the currencies to the pictures of currencies.

Australian dollars (AUD)	British pound (GBP)	Chinese Renminbi (CNY)	Euros (EUR)
Japanese yen (JPY)	Korean won (KRW)	Taiwanese dollar (TWD)	United States dollar (USD)

_____ _____ _____ _____ _____

_____ _____ _____

Sentence Completion

(   ) 1. Daniel: I'd like to make a _____ today. I have some checks I want to add to my savings.
(A) finance   (B) investing   (C) accounting   (D) deposit

(   ) 2. Teller: All right, sir. What is your savings account _____?
(A) number   (B) letter   (C) picture   (D) symbol

(   ) 3. Daniel: It's 1302453. Do I need to fill out a deposit _____ for these checks?
(A) package   (B) permission   (C) slip   (D) reconciliation

(   ) 4. Teller: No, you don't, since you aren't requesting any cash back. Do you have any other _____ I can help you with today?
(A) modifications   (B) transactions   (C) events   (D) steps

(   ) 5. Daniel: Yes, actually. I'd like a(n) _____ card for my checking account. A debit card would be quite useful during those times when I don't have any cash on me and I don't want to write a check.
(A) BAM   (B) APA   (C) ATM   (D) MLA

(   ) 6. Teller: I can help you with that. Would you write out what _____ number you would like for this card? I can program it right onto the card and have it ready for you in a few minutes. The number sequence must be four digits long.
(A) key   (B) pin   (C) classified   (D) user name

Making a withdraw at an ATM 🎧 125

1. Insert your debit or credit card.
2. Enter your personal identification number (PIN).
3. Select "Withdraw" when the ATM prompts you to choose the type of transaction you would like to make.
4. Select the amount of cash you want to withdraw.
5. Take your cash, receipt and card when they come out of the ATM.

Choose it! Use the words in the box to complete the sentences. Change the forms when necessary.

deposit	check	balance	interest	cash

1. I wrote him a _____ for $100.
2. Would you _____ a check for me?
3. I'd like to check my bank _____, please.
4. If you go to the bank, will you _____ these checks for me?
5. You should put the money in a savings account where it will earn _____.

Unit 11

Post Office & Making a Phone Call

◆Language Functions

Post Office & Making a Phone Call

◆Sentence Patterns

Expressions of Sending Mail at a Post Office &
Expressions of Making a Phone Call

◆Vocabulary in Use

Mail-related words & telephone equipment

Part 1   Warm Up

A Check ☑ the following services that the post offices in your country offer.

☐ acceptance of letters and parcels   ☐ sale of postage stamps

☐ provision of post office boxes   ☐ savings accounts

☐ passport applications   ☐ money orders

B Discuss the following questions in a group and then share your ideas with your classmates.

1. What do you think of the postal service in your country?
2. How often do you get real letters – those that are in envelopes and delivered to your door by the postal service?
3. How has the Internet changed the postal service?

Part 2 Dialogues

1. Mailing a letter 127

Postal clerk: Good afternoon, ma'am. How may I help you?

Amy: Good afternoon. I would like to mail a letter please.

Postal clerk: Sure. Where is it going?

Amy: To Taiwan. How much is it for the stamp?

Postal clerk: Will that be standard mail or express mail?

Amy: Uhm, standard mail, please. How much is that?

Postal clerk: Three dollars and sixty-eight cents.

Amy: There you go.

A For each sentence, check ☑ T (true) or F (false)

Word Bank 126

stamp (n.) 郵票
standard (adj.) 標準的
express (adj.) 快遞的

This dialogue takes place at a bank.	T ☐	F ☐
Amy wants to send a parcel to Thailand.	T ☐	F ☐
It will cost Amy $3.68 to send her letter through express mail.	T ☐	F ☐

B Listen to the dialogue again, and then practice with your partner

2. Sending a package 129

Postal clerk: Good morning, sir. How may I help you?

Albert: Good morning. I would like to send a package with some fragile items.

Postal clerk: No problem. We have some boxes here.

Albert: Great. Do you also have bubble wrap?

Postal clerk: Yes, we do.

Albert: OK, I will come back after packing my parcel. Thanks.

Postal clerk: You're welcome.

Albert: Here you are.

(after packing the parcel)

Postal clerk: Thanks. Could you please fill out this form with your name, address, the contents of the box, and the recipient's name and address? Write here in capital letters.

Albert: Sure.

(Albert writing for a while)

Albert: Here you go.

Postal clerk: Alright. Let me weigh your package. It weighs about 8 kilograms.

(Postal clerk weighing for a second)

Albert: Oh, okay. How much do I owe you?

Postal clerk: It's 18 dollars.

Albert: Alright. Here you are.

Postal clerk: Thanks.

Word Bank  128

package (n.) 包裹
fragile (adj.) 易損壞的
item (n.) 項目；品目
bubble (n.) 水泡．氣泡
wrap (n.) 包裹物
pack (v.) 包裝
parcel (n.) 包裹
content (n.) 容納的東西
recipient (n.) 接受者
capital (n.) 大寫字母

A For each sentence, check ☑ T (true) or F (false)

Albert is sending a package with some fragile items.	T ☐	F ☐
The post office doesn't sell boxes for packages.	T ☐	F ☐
Albert's package weighs 18 kilograms.	T ☐	F ☐

B Listen to the dialogue again, and then practice with your partner

Part 3 Sentence Patterns *Expressions of Sending Mail at a Post Office* 🎧 130

I'd like to buy some stamps, please. Five twenty-five-cent and ten ten-cent stamps.

How much does it cost to send a letter / package to Taiwan by air mail / surface mail / registered mail / special delivery?

Are there any fragile items / perishable food items in the package?

I want to send this parcel to Taiwan. Please weigh this parcel for me.

Would you like to insure it against damage or loss?

I'd like to send this parcel insured / I'd like to insure this package, please.

Word Bank 🎧 131

airmail (n.) 航空信
delivery (n.) 投遞
registered (adj.) 掛號的
surface mail (n.) 普通平信郵件
perishable (adj.) 易腐爛的
insure (v.) 為...投保

Now work with your partners to use these sentence patterns to send a parcel at a post office.

Part 4 **Practice**

A Be sure to write neatly when addressing your envelope so your letter will reach its correct destination.

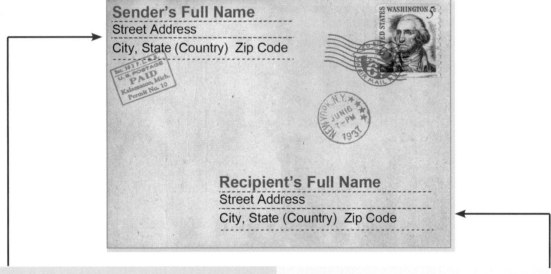

RETURN ADDRESS
This is the information about the sender of the letter. In the top left corner on separate lines write:
Your full name
Your Street Address
Your City, State (or Country) and Zip Code

ADDRESS
This is the name and address of the person (recipient) you are sending the letter to. On separate lines write:
Recipient's Full Name
Street Address
City, State (or Country) and Zip Code

B Now practice addressing an envelope.

Part 5 Role Play

Pair work! Fill in the blanks and practice the completed dialogue with your partner.

Postal clerk   Tourist

🎧 Good morning. May I help you?

👤 I'd like to send this letter by _____ to _____, please.

🎧 Sure. It's _____.

👤 Oh, I nearly forgot. How much is it to send this parcel to _____?

🎧 Do you want to send it by _____ , or by _____?

👤 _____, please.

🎧 Then would you fill _____ this declaration form for customs? Write the contents of the parcel in this space, and mark in this space if it is a gift.

👤 Yes, it is a gift for my _____.

🎧 Also, please write the value of the items in this space.

👤 Is this O.K.?

🎧 Yes, that's fine. That'll be _____ dollars.

Lesson B Making a Phone Call

Part 1 Warm Up

A Match each picture with its name in the following box.

headset	keypad	charger	payphone
touch screen	telephone booth	receiver	SIM card

_____

_____

_____

_____

_____

_____

_____

_____

B When you are making a phone call, what may you say? Check ☑ the correct answers.

☐ This is Frank Chang speaking.　　☐ Can I speak to Ted, please?
☐ I'm calling from San Francisco.　　☐ Can I have extension 232, please?

Part 2 Dialogues

1. **Making a phone call** 133

Receptionist: Good morning, Profit Corporation. May I help you?

Jason: Yes, Jason Chang from Taiwan here. May I speak to Mr. Brian, please?

Receptionist: Mr. Brian is not in right now; can I take a message?

Jason: Yes, please tell him to call me back this afternoon. My number is 345-987-1688.

Receptionist: OK. I'll tell him as soon as he gets in.

Jason: Thank you.

Receptionist: You're welcome.

A For each sentence, check ☑ T (true) or F (false)

> **Word Bank** 🎧 132
>
> message (n.) 口信；信息
> as soon as (phr.) 一... 就...

Mr. Brian is working for the Profit Corporation.	T ☐	F ☐
The receptionist asks Jason to leave a message for Mr. Brian.	T ☐	F ☐
Jason will call Mr. Brian again in the afternoon.	T ☐	F ☐

B Listen to the dialogue again, and then practice with your partner.

Tourism English

2. Making a phone call again 135

Amy: Hello.

Derek: Hello, it's Derek again. Is Angela back yet?

Amy: No, she isn't I'm afraid.

Derek: OK, can I leave a message?

Amy: Of course.

Derek: Could you tell her to call me back when she gets in? I have a new number. It's 0928-588-888.

Amy: Hold on a second. Let me get a pen and paper ......OK, go ahead.

Derek: The number is 0928-588-888. Have you got that?

Amy: OK, let me read that back to you. That's 0928-588-888.

Derek: Yes, that's right.

Amy: Right. I'll make sure she gets your message. Goodbye.

Word Bank 134

hold on (phr.) 不掛電話
go ahead (phr.) 開始

A For each sentence, check ☑ T (true) or F (false)

		T		F	
Derek is calling to Amy.		T ☐		F ☐	
Derek doesn't want to leave a message.		T ☐		F ☐	
Derek's phone number is 0928-885-888		T ☐		F ☐	

B Listen to the dialogue again, and then practice with your partner.

Part 3 Sentence Patterns *Expressions of Making a Phone Call* 🎧136

Can I speak to Mr. Brown, please?
May I ask who's calling? / Could I have your name, please?
Yes, this is Clement Chen speaking.
Could you put me through to Mr. Brown?
Hold the line, / Hold on, please.
I'm afraid his line is engaged. Would you like to leave a message?
Could you ask him to call me back? / Could you ask him to return my call?
Could I leave a message, please? Yes, certainly. / Yes, of course.

A Match the questions on the left coulunm with their answers on the right colunm.

_____ 1. Hello. This is Kenneth Beare. May I speak to Ms. Sunshine, please?

_____ 2. I'm afraid he's out at the moment. Can I take a message?

_____ 3. Could you ask her to meet me at the Capitol 4 movie theatre at 7 pm tonight?

_____ 4. May I know who's calling?

_____ 5. Good Morning. How can I help you?

a. Could I speak to Ms. Simpleton, please?
b. Sure. Just let me write that down.
c. Yes. Can you ask him to give me a call?
d. Hold the line a moment, I'll check if she is in her office.
e. I'm Mohan, David's brother.

B Now practice making a phone call with your partner.

Part 4 Practice

Choose it! Use the words in the box to complete the following paragraph.

call back	directory	reach	wrong number	mine	help
message	got through	speaking	phone number	hold on	

Yesterday I wanted to call my friend Amanda but I couldn't remember her _____, however I knew it began with 0928, so I dialed what I thought could be the right number. Someone answered and said, "Hello, Kenny Rogers _____, Can I _____ you? Oh I said, "Could I speak to Amanda please? She is a friend of _____. Well, Kenny Rogers said, "Can you _____ please, I'll go and tell her someone is asking for her. He came back 5 minutes later and said I'd better _____ in half an hour. I did so and _____ to Kenny Rogers' office again. "Hello." he said, "I'm sorry but there's no Amanda here, you must have dialed a _____. "What a shame!" I said, "I wanted to go out with her tonight but I don't know how to _____ her now! "If you give me some information about her I'll try to check in the _____", Kenny Rogers said. He left me a _____ two hours later, and that was the beginning of our love story.

Part 5 Role Play

Pair work! Fill in the blanks and practice the completed dialog with your partners.

A: Good afternoon, _____, may I help you?

B: Extension _____, please.

A: I'm sorry, the line's _____, will you hold?

B: Yes, I'll hold. ...

A: I'm putting you _____.

C: Marketing, Peter Chang speaking.

B: Could I speak to _____, please?

C: I'm sorry, he's in a meeting _____.

B: Do you know _____?

C: He should be back around five. Can I _____ a message?

B: Yes, please ask him to call _____ on 333-4567.

C: 333-4567, right?

B: That's right.

C: OK, I'll see he gets your message.

Post office box 137

A post office box, often called a P.O. box, is a mailbox located in a central post office where you can opt to receive all or most of your mail. There are some reasons for renting a post office box. If you run a business from your home, you can use it to separate your private mail from your business mail. If people travel frequently, they may also want to rent a P.O. box to collect their mail. If you live in an area where mail gets stolen, it can help to have a box in order to make sure you receive all your mail.

Choose it! Match each picture with its name in the following box.

stamp pad	envelope	mail truck	pillar box
scale	mail carrier	package	stamps

174

Making an International Phone Call  138
In order to make an international phone call,
there are several steps:
Step 1: Dial International Call Prefix
Step 2: Dial Country Code
Step 3: Dial City Code (area code)
Step 4: Dial Local Number
So let's say you are trying to call a local
number in Taoyuan, Taiwan from San
Francisco, California, USA. In this example we will say the local number is 333-4567.
We know that 011 is the internal call prefix when dialing from the USA. The country
code for Taiwan is 886. The city code (or area code) for Taoyuan is 3. This is all the
information we need. To make the call, we would dial 011 886 3 333-4567

Sentence Completion

( ) 1. Oh no! The line is _____
    (A) busy   (B) talking
    (C) holding, she is probably talking to her husband.

( ) 2. Where is your _____.
    (A) answer   (B) free
    (C) directory please? I'd like to find out Maxim's number.

( ) 3. Hold the _____.
    (A) receiver   (B) directory
    (C) line   please, an operator will assist you.

( ) 4. I'm _____
    (A) dialing   (B) speaking
    (C) talking the number of your grandmother.

( ) 5. I don't have any _____.
    (A) answers   (B) questions
    (C) coins for the telephone-box, what can I do ?

Illness & Pains

Unit 12

◆**Language Functions**

Seeing a Doctor & At the Pharmacy

◆**Sentence Patterns**

Expressions of Explaining Health Problems &
Expressions at the Pharmacy

◆**Vocabulary in Use**

Body parts & medical items

Seeing a Doctor

Part 1 Warm Up

A Listen to the following six talks and discuss with your partner what happen to the six persons. 🎧 139

1

I'm feeling ill, I've got quite a bad cough, but I don't seem to have a fever.

What happen to him / her?
_____

2
I've got a headache. I've also had a little bit of diarrhea.

What happen to him / her?
_____

3

My stomach is upset and all I want to do is sleep.

What happen to him / her?
_____

4
I have a sore throat and get tired very quickly.

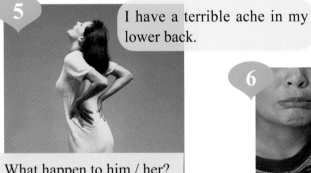

What happen to him / her?
_____

5
I have a terrible ache in my lower back.

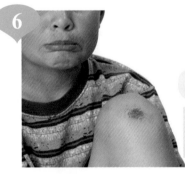

What happen to him / her?
_____

6
My son has hurt his knee.

What happen to him / her?
_____

B What may you say when you are seeing a doctor? Check ☑ the correct answers.

☐ I have a sore throat.   ☐ I feel dizzy when I stand up.
☐ I have been sneezing a lot.   ☐ When did the symptoms start?

Part 2 Dialogues

1. **Booking a doctor's appointment** 141

Receptionist: Doctor's office. How can I help you?

     Caller: I need to make an appointment with Dr. Jackson.

Receptionist: What's your name, please?

     Caller: Albert Chen.

Receptionist: What do you need to see the doctor about?

     Caller: Well, I've been fighting a cold for more than a week, and my cough is getting worse each day.

Receptionist: Hmm. Doctor Jackson is off tomorrow. Do you think it can wait until Thursday?

     Caller: Oh, I hope to get in today or tomorrow.

Receptionist: Actually, we had a cancellation for 3:00 pm today if you can come.

     Caller: Gee, it's almost 2:00 pm already. I think I can make it if I leave right now.

Receptionist: No problem, Mr. Chen. We'll see you in an hour or so.

Word Bank 140

cough (v.) (n.) 咳嗽
actually (adv.) 實際上
cancellation (n.) 取消

A For each sentence, check ☑ **T (true)** or **F (false)**

Albert has a bad cold.	T ☐	F ☐
Albert has an appointment with the doctor on Thursday.	T ☐	F ☐
The doctor will see Albert at 3:00 pm.	T ☐	F ☐

B Listen to the dialogue again, and then practice with your partner.

Tourism English

2. Seeing a doctor 143

Doctor: Good morning. Please have a seat here. What's the problem?

Daniel: I have a terrible cold.

Doctor: Do you have a cough?

Daniel: Yes, I do.

Doctor: Do you have any other symptoms?

Daniel: Yes, I have a sore throat and my nose is stuffy.

Doctor: When did the symptoms start?

Daniel: This morning.

Doctor: I'll check your temperature··· It's OK. You don't have a fever. Please open your mouth wide! Say ah!

(Daniel opens mouth wide)

Doctor: Just as I suspected. It looks like you have got the flu.

Daniel: Can you give me something for the time being?

Doctor: Yes, I'll give you a prescription for cough tablets. Here take this prescription to the pharmacy and get it filled.

> **Word Bank** 142
>
> symptom (n.) 症狀．徵候
> sore (adj.) 痛的；疼痛發炎的
> pharmacy (n.) 藥房
> throat (n.) 喉嚨
> stuffy (adj.) (鼻子) 塞住的
> temperature (n.) 體溫
> fever (n.) 發燒
> flu (n.) 流行性感冒
> prescription (n.) 處方．藥方
> tablet (n.) 藥片
> for the time being (phr.) 目前；暫時

A For each sentence, check ☑ T (true) or F (false)

Daniel has a fever and runny nose.	T ☐	F ☐
Daniel's symptoms started from yesterday evening.	T ☐	F ☐
The doctor gives Daniel a prescription for cough tablets.	T ☐	F ☐

B Listen to the dialogue again, and then practice with your partner.

Part 3 Sentence Patterns *Expressions of Explaining Health Problems* 🎧145

There are two forms we can use to talk about our health problems:

Present perfect continuous: The present perfect continuous is used to show that something started in the past and is still happening now. We use 'I have been + -ing verb.'

I have been coughing a lot these days / recently / for the last few days / since yesterday.

Present simple: The present simple is used to focus on a situation at the present. It is more common to use the present simple than the present continuous when we see a doctor. We use 'I have + noun'

Word Bank 🎧144

diarrhea (n.) 腹瀉
runny nose (phr.) 流鼻涕
toothache (n.) 牙痛
indigestion (n.) 消化不良
dull (adj.) 遲鈍的
chilly (adj.) 冷得使人不舒服的
under the weather(phr.) 身體不舒服

I have a cold / cough / diarrhea / fever / headache / runny nose / sore throat / stomachache / toothache / an indigestion.

also use 'I feel + adjective'

I feel dizzy / dull / sick /chilly / under the weather.

A Discuss with your partner what happen to the following people.

B Use these sentence patterns to describe the health problems you have ever had before.

_____

_____

_____

_____

Part 4 Practice

Medical Information Sheet! Work with your partner to fill out the following form.

Name _____

Personal Information

Full Name: _____   SSN: _____-_____-_____
Address: _____   DOB: ___/___/_____
City/ ST/ Zip: _____   Phone: (____) _____-_____

In Case of Emergency

Contact: _____   Donor: Y / N
Home#:   (____) _____-_____   Directives: _____
Mobile#: (____) _____-_____   _____

Insurance Carrier

Company: _____   ID#: _____
Employer: _____   Group#: _____

Habit

Smoker: _____   Drinks /WK: _____
Blood Type _____   Allergies: _____

Current Medications

Pharmacy Contact Number: (____) _____-_____

Name	Description	Dosage	Purpose

Vitamins / Food Supplements

Name	Description	Dosage	Purpose

Known Conditions, Events, and Previous Surgeries

Date	Event

Current Physicians

Type	Name	Number

Word Bank 🎧 146

SSN= Social Security Number
DOB= Date Of Birth
Directive (n.) 指示；指令

Part 5 Role Play

Pair work! Fill in the blanks and practice the completed dialog with your partner.

Patient   Doctor

What seems to be the _____?

I haven't been feeling well. I have been _____ for the past 8 hours.

I see. And do you _____ a fever?

_____, I checked my _____ one hour ago. It was _____ F.

Hmmm.... Sounds like you got _____. Does your body feel _____?

Yes, my body _____ a little.

OK. I'm going to prescribe an antibiotic... Penicillin...

I'm _____ to Penicillin. Could you prescribe another one?

Oh, OK. I'll prescribe another one. Take one pill every _____ hours, drink plenty of _____, and stay in bed for the next 24 hours.

Thank you, doctor! Where can I buy these pills?

At the Pharmacy

Part 1 Warm Up

A What can you buy at a pharmacy in your country? Circle it!

toiletries

baby products

cosmetics

perfumes

medicines

vegetables

nutrients

suntan lotion

toys

drinks

snacks

caned food

B Have you ever seen strange stuffs sold at a pharmacy? Write them down and share with your classmates.

Part 2 Dialogue

Get medicine at the pharmacy 148

Pharmacist: Hello. Can I help you?

Daniel: Yes, please. I have a prescription. Can you fill it for me?

Pharmacist: Yes. We can do that. Can you wait 5 minutes?

Daniel: Okay.

Pharmacist: Here is your prescription. Have you had this medicine before?

Daniel: No. I haven't. How much can I take?

Pharmacist: It says on the directions that you should take 3 tablets.

Daniel: Okay. 3 tablets. How often should I take it?

Pharmacist: Every 4 hours.

Daniel: Is it safe to take with alcohol?

Pharmacist: No, you can't.

Daniel: Do I need to take it with food?

Pharmacist: It is fine to take it with or without food.

Daniel: Okay. Are there side effects?

Pharmacist: Yes, you may get drowsy. Be careful when you drive.

Daniel: I understand. Thank you.

Pharmacist: You are welcome.

Word Bank 147

medicine (n.) 藥．內服藥
direction (n.) 指示；用法說明
alcohol (n.) 酒精
side effect (phr.) 副作用
drowsy (adj.) 昏昏欲睡的
careful (adj.) 小心的

A For each sentence, check ☑ T (true) or F (false)

Daniel has had the medicine that his doctor prescribed for him before.	T ☐	F ☐
Daniel should take 4 tables of his medicine every 3 hours.	T ☐	F ☐
Daniel is supposed to take the medicine with food.	T ☐	F ☐
The medicine may make Daniel feel sleepy.	T ☐	F ☐

B Listen to the dialogue again, and then practice with your partner.

Part 3 Sentence Patterns *Expressions at the Pharmacy*

150

I've got a prescription here from the doctor.
Are you allergic to any medications? I'm allergic to aspirin.
How should I take this medicine? Take one pill three times a day after meals.
Should I take this with food or without food? You need to take it with food. That's on the label.
Will I have an allergic reaction? Not really. It's very safe.
Are there special side effects that I should look for? Yes, you may get drowsy. Be careful when you drive.

Word Bank 149

allergic (adj.) 過敏的
medication (n.) 藥物治療
pill (n.) 藥丸、藥片
capsule (n.) 膠囊
label (n.) 標籤
reaction (n.) 反應

A Discuss the following medicine label with your partner.

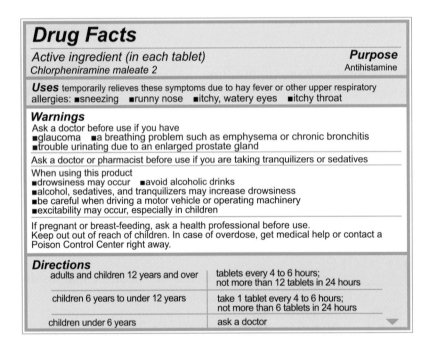

Drug Facts

Active ingredient (in each tablet)	**Purpose**
Chlorpheniramine maleate 2	Antihistamine

Uses temporarily relieves these symptoms due to hay fever or other upper respiratory allergies: ■sneezing ■runny nose ■itchy, watery eyes ■itchy throat

Warnings
Ask a doctor before use if you have
■glaucoma ■a breathing problem such as emphysema or chronic bronchitis
■trouble urinating due to an enlarged prostate gland

Ask a doctor or pharmacist before use if you are taking tranquilizers or sedatives

When using this product
■drowsiness may occur ■avoid alcoholic drinks
■alcohol, sedatives, and tranquilizers may increase drowsiness
■be careful when driving a motor vehicle or operating machinery
■excitability may occur, especially in children

If pregnant or breast-feeding, ask a health professional before use.
Keep out out of reach of children. In case of overdose, get medical help or contact a Poison Control Center right away.

Directions

adults and children 12 years and over	tablets every 4 to 6 hours; not more than 12 tablets in 24 hours
children 6 years to under 12 years	take 1 tablet every 4 to 6 hours; not more than 6 tablets in 24 hours
children under 6 years	ask a doctor

Drug Facts (continued)

Other information ■store at 20-25℃ (68-77℃)   ■protect from excessive moisture

Inactive ingredients D&C yellow no. 10, lactose, magnesium stearate, microcrystalline cellulose, pregelatinized starch

B Now work with your partners to use these sentence patterns to buy medicine

Part 4 **Practice**

Fill it out! Use the words in the box to complete the following paragraph.

warning	prescription	tablets	directions	stomach
pharmacy	dosage	side effects	overdose	pharmacist

I went to the drugstore down the street to fill a _____ at the _____. I have had some problems with my back and the doctor prescribed for me a new medication. I waited in line and when it was my turn, I handed the prescription to the _____. He told me to come back in 10 minutes and he would have it ready for me.

In the meantime, I went to look for some over the counter stomach medication. There was some in _____ and capsules. I decided on the capsules and returned to the pharmacy.

The pharmacist asked me if I had taken this medication before. I told him I hadn't, and he pointed out the _____ on the bottle. It had the _____ information: Take three tablets three times a day. There was also a _____ to not take it on an empty _____. The bottle also said that I should stop taking the medication if I had any serious _____. The pharmacist told me to follow the directions closely so that I can avoid an _____. I paid for the medication and thanked him for his help.

Part 5 Role Play

Pair work! Fill in the blanks and practice the completed dialogue with your partner.

Pharmacist: Hello. Can I help you?

Customer: Yes, please. I have _____. Can you fill it for me?

Pharmacist: Yes. We can do that. It'll take just _____ minutes, sir.

Customer: Okay.

Pharmacist: Here is your _____ .

Customer: Thank you. How much can I take?

Pharmacist: Take _____ tablet(s) _____ times a day.

Customer: Okay. _____ tablet(s) _____ times a day. Is it safe to take with _____?

Pharmacist: _____, you _____.

Customer: I understand. Thank you.

Pharmacist: You are welcome.

Talk to your doctor 152

Be sure to tell your doctor about any current and past health care issues or concerns. It's important to share any information you can, even if you're embarrassed. Give your doctor the following information during the exam:

1. Any symptoms you are having.
2. Your health history.
3. Any medicines you are currently taking. Include information about when and how often you take the medicine.
4. Any side effects you have from your medicine, especially if it makes you feel sick or if you think you may be allergic to it.

Word Bank 151

current (adj.) 現時的
past (adj.) 過去的
concern (n.) 關心的事
embarrassed (adj.) 尷尬的
exam (n.) 檢查
especially (adv.) 尤其

Recognize your body! Use the words in the box to fill in the following picture.

shoulder	elbow
forehead	arm
ankle	finger
chest	nose
knee	neck

Word Bank 151

dentist (n.) 牙醫
obstetrician (n.) 產科醫師
optometrist (n.) 驗光師・視光師
pediatrician (n.) 小兒科醫師
surgeon (n.) 外科醫生
general practitioner (n.) 全科醫師

Match it! Match each word with its definition.

1. Dentist
2. Obstetrician
3. Optometrist
4. Pediatrician
5. Surgeon
6. General Practitioner

a. An eye doctor
b. A family doctor who you would usually go to see for common health problems
c. A doctor for female patients before and during pregnancy (child birth).
d. A doctor who performs operations
e. A doctor for children
f. A doctor who treats teeth

The steps of getting medicine  153

In the United States of America, your doctor just gave you a prescription, what should you do?

1. Take your prescription to a nearby pharmacy or drugstore.
2. The pharmacist will need the prescription. In order to fill a prescription, the pharmacist must have the name, city, state, phone and fax number of the doctor that prescribed it.
3. The pharmacist will also ask about any allergies and general medical conditions.
4. The pharmacist will ask if you have an insurance card. Show your insurance card to the pharmacist.
5. The pharmacist calls your name when the prescription is ready. Walk up to the pharmacy counter and talk with the pharmacist. Make sure you understand all the directions.

Choose it! Match each picture with its name in the following box.

| stethoscope | heart monitor | thermometer | syringe |
| capsules | crutches | bandages | pills |

_____ _____ _____ _____

_____ _____ _____ _____

Tourism English

作　　者	陳祖昱
審　　閱	戴芳美
發 行 人	陳本源
執行編輯	游智帆
封面設計	楊昭琅
出 版 者	全華圖書股份有限公司
郵政帳號	0100836-1 號
印 刷 者	宏懋打字印刷股份有限公司
圖書編號	08152017
二版三刷	2019 年 10 月
定　　價	390 元
Ｉ Ｓ Ｂ Ｎ	978-986-463-052-3

全華圖書 / www.chwa.com.tw

全華網路書店 Open Tech / www.opentech.com.tw

若您對書籍內容、排版印刷有任何問題，歡迎來信指導 book@chwa.com.tw

臺北總公司（北區營業處）

地址：23671 新北市土城區忠義路 21 號

電話：(02) 2262-5666

傳眞：(02) 6637-3695、6637-3696

南區營業處

地址：80769 高雄市三民區應安街 12 號

電話：(07) 381-1377

傳眞：(07) 862-5562

中區營業處

地址：40256 臺中市南區樹義一巷 26 號

電話：(04) 2261-8485

傳眞：(04) 3600-9806

✂（請由此線剪下）

歡迎加入 全華會員

● 會員獨享

會員享購書折扣、紅利積點、生日禮金、不定期優惠活動…等。

● 如何加入會員

填妥讀者回函卡直接傳真(02) 2262-0900 或寄回，將由專人協助登入會員資料，待收到 E-MAIL 通知後即可成為會員。

如何購買 全華書籍

1. 網路購書

全華網路書店「http://www.opentech.com.tw」，加入會員購書更便利，並享有紅利積點回饋等各式優惠。

2. 全華門市、全省書局

歡迎至全華門市（新北市土城區忠義路21號）或全省各大書局、連鎖書店選購。

3. 來電訂購

(1) 訂購專線：(02) 2262-5666 轉 321-324
(2) 傳真專線：(02) 6637-3696
(3) 郵局劃撥（帳號：0100836-1 戶名：全華圖書股份有限公司）
※ 購書未滿一千元者，酌收運費70元。

OpenTech.com.tw 全華網路書店

全華網路書店 www.opentech.com.tw
E-mail: service@chwa.com.tw

※ 本會員制如有變更則以最新修訂制度為準，造成不便請見諒。